WORDS GET
IN THE WAY

**Center Point
Large Print**

**This Large Print Book carries the
Seal of Approval of N.A.V.H.**

WORDS GET IN THE WAY

NAN ROSSITER

CENTER POINT LARGE PRINT
THORNDIKE, MAINE

For my mom and dad

This Center Point Large Print edition
is published in the year 2012 by arrangement with
Kensington Publishing Corp.

The text of this Large Print edition is unabridged.
In other aspects, this book may vary
from the original edition.
Printed in the United States of America
on permanent paper.
Set in 16-point Times New Roman type.

ISBN: 978-1-61173-384-6

Library of Congress Cataloging-in-Publication Data

Rossiter, Nan Parson.
Words get in the way / Nan Rossiter. — Large print ed.
p. cm. — (Center Point large print edition)
ISBN 978-1-61173-384-6 (lib. bdg. : alk. paper)
1. Mothers and sons—Fiction. 2. Autistic children—Fiction.
  3. Farm life—Fiction. 4. Families—Fiction. 5. Domestic fiction.
  6. Large type books. I. Title.
PS3618.O8535W67 2012
813'.6—dc23
                                                    2012005412

ACKNOWLEDGMENTS

I can hardly believe that I've been given the opportunity to write a second novel! When I was writing my first, and praying it would be published, I promised God I would try to write uplifting stories that make a difference. I hope readers find *Words Get in the Way* to be that kind of story.

When I began writing, a young mom from our church, Krista Dirienzo, introduced me to her young son Joey. Krista shared with me the heartache of the moment she learned that Joey has autism, and she told me about some of the revealing traits. Krista's openness and willingness to answer all of my questions were a tremendous help, and Joey's sweet personality was my beginning inspiration for Henry.

When I was almost finished writing, a young man named Michael Smith serendipitously sat next to me at a book signing for one of my children's books. Michael showed me a notebook filled with his amazing drawings and then began to share with me what it's like to *have* autism. Michael thoughtfully considered and answered all of my questions and, when he wasn't sure of an answer, he encouraged me to ask his parents.

To my wonderful agent, Deirdre Mullane,

whose guidance is invaluable and who always has a word of encouragement.

To my awesome editor, Audrey LaFehr, and everyone on the Kensington team, who believe in me and who, together, do their very best to make every book a success.

To my husband, Bruce, and our sons, Cole and Noah, the handsome men who inspire me and who always keep me smiling!

And to all of my reading friends: I have been overwhelmed by the support from readers across the country—and especially those in my community—from coverage in the local papers to, every time I'm in town, someone stopping to say, "I'm reading your book!" or "Our book club is doing your book!" or my favorite compliment: "You kept me up all night!"

Thank you all! I am truly blessed.

PROLOGUE

Callie stood by the window, watching the late-day sun play hide-and-seek with the clouds. The buses began to pull away, and as the last one passed, she noticed a small blond head leaning against one of the windows, peering out. The little boy looked weary as he gazed through the glass, but when he saw her standing there he sat up, beaming, and opened and closed his small fist. Callie smiled and waved back.

She continued to watch as the buses disappeared and then turned to straighten up her classroom. She picked up pencils and crayons and put chairs up on desks so Jim could vacuum. When she came to the desk of the little boy on the bus, though, she paused. Shy Sam, as she called him, always remembered to put his chair up; he even put his neighbors' chairs up when they forgot. She pictured his sweet smile and thought of Henry when he was that age. Sam was quiet, was meticulously neat, and loved to draw, and Callie often thought he must be cut from the same cloth as Henry.

She took down Sam's chair, sat in it with her knees touching the underside of his desk, and opened his crayon box. Sam organized his crayons by color, just as Henry had always done, and Callie knew that every crayon was accounted for, even the ones that had become too short to hold. She closed the box, slipped it back in his desk, and looked at the drawing he'd been working on that day. It was a picture of Winston, his beloved golden retriever. She smiled, remembering all the pictures Henry had drawn of Springer. *Sweet old Springer!*

Callie gazed out the window at the now-gray sky. She couldn't believe Henry was going to be sixteen that winter. *Where has the time gone?* She could still picture him with his arm around Springer's neck. And she could still remember, with vivid clarity, the fateful week thirteen years earlier when their lives had changed forever.

PART I

Something there is that doesn't love a wall,
That sends the frozen-ground-swell under it
And spills the upper boulders in the sun . . .

—Robert Frost

I

Callie knelt beside Henry's bed. He looked so peaceful, so different from the frustrated little boy she lived with all day. She reached over and lightly brushed the wisps of blond hair from his forehead. She watched him breathe, his lips slightly parted; she marveled at the smallness of his perfect hands and stroked his smooth cheek. Henry murmured and pulled his beloved Travelin' Bear closer until the worn stuffed animal was tucked tightly under his chest. She whispered his prayer for him, as she always did, leaned forward, kissed him gently, and breathed in his sweet little boy scent. Finally, the tears she'd been fighting all day spilled hotly down her cheeks. She slumped against his bed, buried her face in her arms, and cried into the soft cotton sheets. She listened to the thunderstorm rumbling into the valley and, for the hundredth time that day, silently pleaded, *Please don't let this be true. Please make Henry better. Just make it go away. Don't punish Henry for the things I've done.*

Callie stayed beside Henry's bed for a long time before finally pulling herself up and collapsing on the bed in the next room. She was exhausted, but sleep eluded her as she stared into the darkness and replayed the foolish encounter that had changed her life. At the time it had seemed so innocent. Afterward, though, she knew there had been nothing innocent in the events that led to that night.

It was a sunny Tuesday when they'd first met for coffee to discuss her thesis. The following Friday, it had been a beer at an outdoor pub on Church Street to celebrate the arrival of spring. And on Saturday, he had appeared handsome and smiling to take her to dinner at a quiet inn on Lake Champlain. They'd sat on the porch and watched the lights around the lake begin to flicker and sparkle as the sun streaked radiant flames of color across the sky. They'd shared a bottle of Merlot and talked about her plans for graduate school and his hope for tenure. Then he'd ordered a second bottle, and Callie had begun to wonder what he was thinking. She had watched him toy with the gold band on his finger and thought of Linden. *What would he think if he saw me now?* She had pushed the thought away.

He had paid for dinner, carefully eased the cork back into the second bottle, and discreetly smuggled it out under his tweed jacket, and then he'd jovially draped his arm over her shoulder as they'd made their way back to his car. Driving a short distance, he had pulled into the parking lot of a secluded beach. When he'd opened the back of his Volvo wagon and produced a wool stadium blanket, it had suddenly seemed too convenient. Callie had felt an unsettling wave of apprehension. *This has already gone too far.* At the same time, she hadn't tried to stop it.

They'd sat on the blanket and he'd laughed as he struggled with the bottle between his legs and she'd laughed too as she tried to help by holding it while he pulled on the cork. Finally it had eased out, splashing a spot of red wine on his khaki pants. He had run his finger around the top to wipe off any stray droplets and, with a smile, passed the bottle to her. She'd hesitated, smiling too, but finally she'd taken a sip, her heart pounding.

As they watched the lights dance on the water, he'd slipped his jacket off and dropped it over her shoulders. Passing the wine back and forth had reminded Callie of high school. And then he'd brushed his hand along her thigh and teased her about having only one dimple and, feeling light-headed, she'd grinned mischievously, slowly running the tip of her tongue around the lip of the bottle.

He had watched with raised eyebrows. "Where'd you learn that, Miss Wyeth?"

"Learn what?" Callie had asked, feigning innocence.

"Hmmm, what else do you know?" His eyes had sparkled as he'd lightly traced his finger around her dimple and along her lips, and Callie had closed her eyes and let him.

Callie hated the memory, but sometimes it slipped into her mind, and she couldn't seem to stop it. Two months later she'd discovered she was pregnant, but when she tried to reach him at the college they told her that he had taken a job in California. *Whatever happened to tenure?* she'd wondered bitterly.

Callie finally drifted off, but it seemed like it was only moments before she awakened to the sound of crying. In the early morning light she found Henry rocking back and forth on the floor. She scooped him up, felt him shiver in her arms, and pulled the blanket around him. He continued to whimper, and she whispered softly into his tousled hair, "It's okay, Hen-Ben, everything's going to be okay." Her words of reassurance were as much for herself as they were for him.

She glanced around the room at the pile of boxes and sighed. She knew the unfamiliar surroundings weren't helping Henry, but there was nothing else she could do. Without childcare she was unable to work, and she had no money left. In the half light of dawn she stared at a box labeled "Henry / LEGOs" and relived the last few months.

During that time she'd noticed a change in Henry but she'd convinced herself it was nothing to worry about. *He's just quiet, that's all. Some boys just develop more slowly than others and, besides, Henry knows how to use words. . . . He already started to.* Callie tried to remember the last time Henry had actually spoken. *That's okay,* she had told herself, *he'll learn when he's ready*. All of Callie's self-reassuring, however, had gone right out the window when Mrs. Cooper had voiced her concern too.

Mrs. Cooper was the matriarch of the daycare near the college—the daycare where Callie had been leaving Henry since he was six months old. After he was born, she'd been unable to continue her studies and had instead taken a job in the financial aid office. She'd always felt blessed and thankful to have found such a wonderful home away from home for Henry, and she could still see the faded green carpet and the pattern of shadows from the windows that crisscrossed the floor of the large playroom every afternoon when she picked him up. On that last afternoon Callie had been waiting for him by the door when Mrs. Cooper had taken her aside. She remembered the concern in her voice as she'd quietly told her that she'd been watching Henry for several weeks and been praying for a positive sign.

"Henry is so quiet," she'd said, "and often he just seems lost. Lately, he shows no interest in playing with other children. Instead, he just stands at the rice table and pours rice from one cup to another or lets the rice pour through his hands. If another child interrupts him or borrows one of his cups, he becomes very agitated. Just today, another boy took the cup he was using and gave him a different one. Henry became very upset and erupted into an inconsolable tantrum. He threw all the toys that were on the rice table as well as handfuls of Legos. When he finally calmed down," Mrs. Cooper continued, "I asked him to join our reading group, but he refused and just sat in the corner, rocking back and forth. I'm so sorry, Callie, I wanted to be sure before I said anything."

Callie had been staring at the pattern on the carpet when a passing cloud drifted in front of the sun. She'd nodded slowly, tears stinging her eyes. "I think you need to have Henry tested, dear," Mrs. Cooper had said kindly, giving her a hug. "Please let us know how you make out. We will be keeping both of you in our prayers." Callie realized then that Mrs. Cooper was saying she would no longer be able to look after Henry.

Callie pressed her cheek into Henry's wispy hair and realized he'd fallen asleep. She laid him down and tucked the soft blanket around him. As tired as she was, there was no point in going back to bed. Besides, she could get so much done if he kept sleeping so she slipped quietly from the room that had once been hers, left the door open a crack, and shuffled barefoot to the kitchen to see if her dad had any coffee. She opened the cabinet next to the sink where her parents had always kept it, and there it was, in the same spot as always, a dark blue can of Maxwell House. The sight of the familiar can in its proper place gave Callie an odd feeling of comfort. As she reached for it, though, she became acutely aware of the emptiness of her parents' house. The people she loved most in the world were no longer there and never would be again, to make coffee, to cradle warm cups in their hands, to chat over breakfast, to talk about the day ahead, and then hurry out the door to school, to work, with a kiss and a promise. . . . *Love you! Keep the faith! See you tonight!* Their lovely voices echoed through her mind. Callie looked out the kitchen window of her childhood home and tears filled her eyes. She had never felt more alone.

2

Linden Finch rolled up the windows of his old Ford pickup and climbed out. He was late getting home, but the summer storm that the weatherman had promised was right on time. A sudden gust of wind swayed the trees ominously and hastened his step. Two yellow Labs that had been chasing squirrels and lazing on the porch all day spied his arrival, rose from their slumber, stretched, and trotted happily across the yard to greet him. Linden knelt down to say hello. "How was your day?" he asked softly. They responded by wiggling all around him, licking his face, and beating his head with their tails. A rumble in the distance caused Linden to stand and look at the wall of threatening clouds that was forming across the meadow. As he did, a ragged streak of hot white light divided the sky. Out of a boyhood habit, he began to silently count the seconds from light to sound but only reached "one-Mississippi" when he heard the rumble again. He hurried to the barn and clicked the latch for two Randall cows that were lowing impatiently at the gate. They nudged their warm noses into his chest as they trundled by into the safety of their stalls and then continued their expectant lowing. A little mule followed them and moseyed into its own stall. Linden flipped up the switch inside the door, and the barn filled with a warm, cheerful light. The dogs plowed their snouts through the hay on the floor while Linden fed and watered the cows and the little mule, talking softly to them the whole time. The younger dog lifted his nose onto a bale of hay and snorted at Maude, the orange tiger cat that was slumbering peacefully there. She opened one eye and studied him indifferently while Harold, her silky dark gray counterpart, yawned and stretched on the bale above her. Linden hurried outside to check the henhouse. As usual, all of the ladies were already nestled down for the night, so he quietly closed the door and latched it.

Fat drops of rain began to splatter on the dry earth as he ducked back into the barn. He looked up into the rafters at the old speckled owl, and it blinked back at him. Linden switched off the light and called the dogs to his side, and together they peered out into the yard. As if on cue, the skies opened up. Linden quickly calculated the distance between the barn and the porch *and* how wet they were going to get. "Let's go!" he shouted, and dashed across the yard. The dogs followed gleefully, splashing through every puddle they could find along the way.

In the shelter of the kitchen Linden pulled off his wet shirt, hung it over the back of a chair, reached for a dish towel, dried his hair with it, and then toweled off the two dogs that were still wiggling around him. He threw the towel on the washer, opened the fridge, grabbed a beer, and headed for the pantry in the back of the kitchen. The dogs followed and plopped down obediently as he measured a cup of kibble into each of their bowls. Linden hesitated, and Springer stared longingly at his food while Kat watched Linden. He nodded to her and, for Springer's sake, said the word, "Okay!" Springer lunged at his bowl as if he hadn't eaten in a week, but Kat made a vain attempt to be more ladylike. Linden shook his head. He slipped the beer bottle into the metal bottle opener mounted on the doorjamb, pulled on it, caught the cap, and stepped back out onto the porch to watch the storm. He dropped into one of the old wicker chairs, ran his hand through his wet hair, and breathed in the rain-soaked air. As the storm rumbled by, he remembered seeing the lights on in the Wyeth place and wondered if something had happened. Mr. Wyeth had been in a nursing home for six months now, but Linden had recently heard that his health had taken a turn for the worse.

The storm passed quickly, and Linden realized that the dogs were peering out through the screen door. He pulled himself from the chair and, when he opened the door, they greeted him again as if he were a long-lost friend, and then followed him happily into the kitchen to see what *he* was going to have for supper. Linden put a small frying pan on the stovetop to heat up leftover spaghetti and washed and sliced an early tomato. He dropped a juicy chunk in his mouth, sifted through his mail, and discovered a check for a job he'd finished two months earlier. After dinner, he washed the dishes, let the dogs out, gave them each a treat, shut off the lights, and headed for bed.

In the half darkness, he threw his jeans over the back of a chair and his T-shirt onto a growing pile of laundry in the hamper. He pushed his bedroom window up and listened to the familiar call of a barred owl. He recognized it as the voice of his faithful barn dweller, and then, somewhere in the distance, he heard a haunting reply of interest. A cool breeze rustled the curtains as Linden lay back on his bed and, for the first time in a long time, he allowed an image of Callie to slip into his mind. It was the same image that always came to him, when he let it, like a favorite photograph his mind kept under glass.

She was smiling and reaching up to push back wisps of wild, wavy hair that the wind had swept across her cheeks. She was wearing a snow-white tank top over her red lifeguard suit, and her shoulders were the golden tan of summer's end. Linden didn't know why he always pictured Callie that way. It had been four years, but after seeing the lights on in her parents' house, he couldn't help but wonder if she had finally come home. With the image still in his mind he drifted to sleep.

Before dawn, he awoke to the loud racket of his squirrel-proof birdfeeder hitting the ground, followed by angry squabbling. He suddenly remembered what he'd forgotten to do: take the birdfeeder down for the night. "Damn those raccoons!" he grumbled as he kicked off his sheet, stumbled to the back door in his boxers, and turned on the light. "Get out of here!" he growled, opening and slamming the door to show them he meant business. "One of these days I will outsmart *or* shoot you!" he added. The dogs thumped their tails agreeably and looked up, wondering if it might be time for breakfast. He looked at them and immediately knew what they were thinking. "No, it's not," he grumbled, falling back onto his bed. But it was useless; he knew he wouldn't be able to fall back asleep.

He got up, pulled on his worn Levis, shuffled barefoot to the kitchen, reached for an almost-empty bag of Green Mountain coffee, and turned on the radio just in time to hear the recorded chorus of songbirds that the program's host, Robert J. Lurtsema, always played at the opening of his broadcast. Most of the time the WGBH signal wasn't strong enough to carry all the way to New Hampshire, but on rare occasions, it came in as clear as a bell. Linden smiled and wondered if his parents, perpetually early risers, were listening in their Boston home. His mother loved classical music and, to placate her, Linden had endured eight long years of piano lessons. At one time he could play everything from Beethoven's *Für Elise* to selections from Bach's complex *Das Wohltemperierte Klavier*, but, just to drive her crazy, he'd also been known to launch into a rousing rendition of the theme from *Gilligan's Island* or Elton John's version of "Pinball Wizard." His mother had fumed, "I knew we should have insisted on private school!" In the end, Linden had prevailed, his mother had relented, and he was allowed to give up the lessons.

Pachelbel's Canon drifted softly from the radio as he poured steaming coffee into the cream-colored mug he liked to use. The mug was adorned with a faded painting of a lighthouse on its side and was one of several items, including an old Chevy pickup, that the cabin's owner and previous resident had left behind. Linden took a sip, gazed out the window at the mist rising from the north-running Contoocook River, and, in spite of everything, felt oddly content.

3

Callie could almost hear her father's voice. *Keep your chin up, kiddo! It's not the end of the world!* In spite of herself, she smiled as she poured coffee into her father's favorite mug and ran her finger over the faded U.S. Navy anchor painted on its side. She sat at the kitchen table and noticed that his Bible was tucked under some papers. She wondered why he hadn't taken it with him. She reached for it and discovered that a copy of *The Upper Room* was still tucked between its pages. For as long as Callie could remember, her parents had faithfully taken the time every morning to read the little magazine's suggested Bible verse and daily devotional. She had even picked up the habit for a while when she was in high school, and she'd often been surprised when the words seemed to speak to whatever challenge she was facing at the time. Afterward, when she went off to college, her mom had continued to send the magazine to her, but she'd rarely found the time to read it.

She slipped the magazine out of the Bible and

glanced at the open date, January 15, two days before her dad had moved to the nursing home. She thought of the call she'd received from his attorney around that time to see if she could come home and arrange to have the house drained. He had explained that it would save on the heating bill, but Callie had never found the time. She'd visited her dad as often as she could, but she'd purposely avoided stopping by the house. If she had, she realized now, she would have found his Bible sooner. She picked it up and put it by the door. She would stop at the church to pick up a current copy of *The Upper Room* and bring it when they went to visit him later.

Reaching over the sink, Callie pushed on the gray metal bracket that slid the bottom of the kitchen window out, but it was stubbornly stuck so she climbed up on the counter, as she'd done when she was little, and put all of her weight behind it. It creaked and, reluctantly, slid out, releasing a rush of fresh morning air into the musty kitchen. She moved to the living room and pushed open those windows too, and then she tugged open the heavy wooden front door and discovered she needed to locate the screen inserts for the storm door.

She dressed quietly, pulled her blond hair back into a ponytail, peeked in on Henry, and took her cup of coffee outside. Standing in the garage doorway, she contemplated the pile of boxes that were waiting in the back of her dad's pickup truck and sighed. For someone with so little money she had certainly accumulated a lot of stuff. She started the truck, pulled it out into the sun, and began to unload.

Henry opened his eyes and quickly shut them again. Each time he opened them, he hoped he would see a wooden bookcase in front of a blue wall. On the shelf of the bookcase, which had a long scratch on one side, should be six books lined up in order of height and, next to the books, a model of a truck that he'd made from LEGOs and, beside that, a small Model M John Deere tractor. But each time he opened his eyes, he quickly shut them again because what he expected to see wasn't there. He really needed to pee too. Finally, unable to hold it in any longer, he just lay there and let it stream out. At first it felt warm but, after a while, it felt cold and he began to cry.

Callie carried the last box inside. As she put it on the kitchen counter she heard a muffled sound, hurried down the hall, and found Henry sitting on the floor in wet underpants with his arms around his knees. "Oh, honey, I'm sorry." She helped him stand and guided him across the hall. "Why didn't you look for the bathroom?" Henry rubbed his eyes and, at her suggestion, looked around.
    She continued to talk to him as she filled the tub

with warm water. She bathed him quickly and, since the water seemed to calm him, let him play for a few minutes while she went to pull the wet sheets off the bed. When she returned to lift him out, though, he kicked and screamed. Callie set him down again, disappeared, and returned with a toy truck, hoping the distraction would work. While Henry inspected the truck, she lifted him out again and gently dried him with the soft towel. Then she rinsed the tub and headed down the hall to look for a box of clothes. Wearing the towel caped over his shoulders and clutching the truck in his hands, Henry traipsed down the hall after her.

"Did you know this used to be Mommy's room?" she asked as she rummaged through one of the boxes. Henry solemnly furrowed his brow as he looked around the small, simply furnished room. He pointed to the pine bureau, and she turned to see what had caught his eye. Lined up in front of her mirror were several old trophies. Callie tugged clean underwear, shorts, and a T-shirt from a bulging box of clothes; tucked them under her arm; picked up one of the trophies; and knelt down in front of him. Henry traced his finger lightly over the figure of a girl shooting a basketball and left a shiny gold trail through the years of settled dust. Callie handed the trophy to him to hold while she pulled on his shorts, and Henry put his free hand on her shoulder as he lifted each leg. When she pulled his T-shirt over his head, he put the trophy down and slipped his arms through. Once he was dressed, he picked the trophy up again and ran his finger over the engraved nameplate. "Let's see which one you have," she said, pausing to read the inscription. " 'Most Dedicated.' Seems like forever ago." Henry pointed to the trophy of a girl kicking a soccer ball and then one of a girl swinging a bat. Callie patiently handed all of her high school trophies to him and watched as he carefully lined them up in order of height. "You're a funny guy," she said with a gentle smile. Henry looked up and pointed to a medal that was hanging from the corner of the mirror. As Callie reached for it she noticed a faded photo tucked into the mirror's frame. She handed the medal to Henry, slipped out the photo, and sat down next to him. While Henry examined his new treasure, Callie looked at the tall, slender boy in the photo and recalled a long-ago summer day.

It had been the last day before they'd headed off to different colleges, a decision his parents had pressed hard for. That morning, she'd finally started getting her things together when he'd surprised her by stopping by to see if she wanted to go hiking. He'd even packed a picnic lunch. She had surveyed the piles of clothes on her bed and then the look on his face, and had reluctantly given in.

The New Hampshire air had whispered of

autumn, and Callie remembered thinking that she'd never seen a sky so blue. They'd hiked to the summit of Monadnock, and after lunch he'd stood to find the mountain's benchmark. Callie had slipped her camera out of her pack and called to him, and he'd looked over his shoulder. Seeing the camera, he'd mustered a half smile. In the photo his chestnut hair was streaked from the sun and windblown from hiking and his face was tan, but the camera had also captured a measure of sadness in his eyes.

Henry reached up and put the medal around Callie's neck and then pointed at the boy in the picture. Callie smiled wistfully and whispered, "Linden."

After she'd taken the photo, Linden had pulled her into his arms, and she'd tried to catch his eye but he'd looked away.

"What's the matter?" she'd asked.

"Nothing," he'd murmured, his eyes glistening in the sunlight.

"It doesn't seem like nothing."

He had looked up at the endless blue sky and stammered, "I hope you know how much I'm going to miss you." Finally, he had turned to her and searched her eyes. "Callie, please don't forget about us."

"Linden, don't you know?" she'd whispered. "I could *never* forget about us."

Callie shook her head sadly, slipped the picture

back into the mirror's frame, and went down the hall to the linen closet to look for clean sheets. At the bottom of a neatly stacked pile she found an old threadbare set that had once been hers and a clean mattress pad. She pulled them out, went back to her room, put the mattress pad on, shook open the fitted bottom sheet, stretched it over the corners of the mattress, and recalled how she'd always begged her mom to just wash the sheets and put them back on instead of putting on different ones. Henry pointed to the figures on the faded pillowcase and Callie nodded. "Yup, Mickey and Minnie, and on the other side," she said, turning the pillow over, "is Donald and Daisy." Henry looked at Donald and Daisy and then turned the pillow back over so Mickey and Minnie were on top. After the bed was made, Callie took the laundry basket to the basement and threw a load in her parents' old Kenmore, shaking out the last of the Tide from a damp box that was on the floor. She trudged back up the stairs, wondering if there was anything in the cabinet that they could have for breakfast. She found Henry lining up the kitchen chairs in a neat row, and she scooped him up. "What in the world are you doing, Hen-Ben?" she asked with a smile. But Henry squirmed and fussed, so she set him down again. She opened the cereal cabinet and found a box of stale Shredded Wheat and an old box of chocolate Carnation Instant Breakfast, neither of which would be very good without milk. She clicked off the coffeepot, picked up her dad's Bible, turned to Henry. "We're going to see Papa," she announced. To her surprise, Henry left the chairs without a fuss.

After stopping at the church to pick up an *Upper Room*, Callie pulled into McDonald's and realized they were already serving lunch. She reached into her pocket, pulled out three singles, and ordered a Happy Meal. She wasn't very hungry, and besides, she knew she'd end up with at least one McNugget and some fries. She definitely needed to ask her dad if she could borrow some money though.

As they drove along, Callie thought about the nursing home and wondered if her dad might be able to move back home now that she was there. His care wouldn't be easy, but it would make him so much happier. The idea bolstered her mood and gave her hope.

The air in the lobby of the nursing home was stale and old. She stopped in front of the elevator and remembered the scene Henry had made the last time they'd used it. Its close quarters or its unfamiliar movement had upset him, so, not wanting to cause another scene, she lifted him onto her hip and climbed the three flights of stairs instead. Taking two at a time, she had to stop on the second landing to tuck the Bible more tightly under her arm. On the third landing she pushed open the door, stepped into the hall, and walked quickly past the ghostly quiet rooms, trying not to notice all of the forgotten souls as they passed. It broke her heart to see so many lonely old folks, and she wondered how anyone could work there, day after day. Some patients were in wheelchairs and their heads were drooped so low that their chins rested on their chests; it was almost as if, after so many years, their heads had become too heavy to hold up. Other patients pushed walkers along slowly with no apparent destination, and one old fellow with no teeth called out, "Hey, cutie, can you give me a ride home?" Callie smiled sadly, shook her head, and continued on. As she approached her dad's room, a nurse emerged with sheets in her arms but, seeing Callie, stopped abruptly.

"Miss Wyeth, we've been trying to reach you." Callie saw the concerned look on her face and her heart began to pound.

"Is he okay?" she blurted.

"He is . . ." The nurse paused and put her hand on Callie's arm. "He had a mild stroke last night. We tried to reach you at both of the numbers we have on file, but we only got recordings saying they've been disconnected."

Callie started to pull away. "Yes, I know. They turned our phone on, but it's still not working. They're supposed to come out next week and fix it." She turned to go into her dad's room, but the nurse stopped her.

"Miss Wyeth, your father isn't here. He was rushed to the hospital last night."

4

Linden loved stone walls, and although he understood the sentiment in Robert Frost's poem, he took umbrage with the poet's choice of metaphor. To Linden the act of building a stone wall was an art form, an architectural ritual, a puzzle to be solved, a time for meditation, and, quite possibly, a simple path to redemption. Linden felt at peace when he was working on a wall. He held each stone in his hands, feeling its weight and texture, tracing his fingers over its lines and moss, and thinking about the hands that had held it last; perhaps they were the tough, calloused hands of a farmer, or maybe they were the smooth, knowing hands of a Native American scout. Only the stone knew the touch that had lifted it into place or carelessly tossed it aside. And from snow cover to sunlight, from swirl of autumn leaf to relentless pelting rain, the stones had weathered the world and its storms and endured to sparkle again in the dancing shafts of sunlight that filtered through the trees. Carefully choosing each stone, Linden felt as if he became a part of its story.

The words of the poem ran through his mind as he laid the last stone on the Connors' wall and stepped back. "Looks good," a voice bellowed. Linden turned and saw Mr. Connor walking toward him. "Just in time too!" He held an envelope out to Linden and, in a thick Boston accent, said, "The less the govahment knows, the bettah!" He stepped back to admire Linden's handiwork. "Very nice!" he said, clapping Linden on the shoulder. "Ahh expect to see you at the picnic this yeaah." Linden smiled, and they both looked up as Mrs. Connor crossed the lawn with a plate in her hands. Overhearing her husband she chimed in, "The boys'll be home, and Katie too."

The boys were the Connors' twin sons, Josh and Jon, classmates of Linden's, and now, Linden knew, well on their way to high-paying careers in finance. Katie was the youngest Connor, a strawberry-blond, freckle-faced tomboy who had never tried to hide the crush she had on Linden. He smiled at the thought of Katie. She'd always been a good sport and seemed to understand that his heart belonged to Callie.

"How is Katie?" he asked.

"Oh, fine, fine," Mr. Connor answered, "just finished her junyaah year at Dahtmouth."

Linden shook his head in disbelief. "She's going to be a senior?!"

"Yup, time flies! Now, don't go changing the subject. . . . Back to the Fauth. There'll be lots of food, as always, and fireworks of course. I think the whole town is coming!"

"We invited your parents, Linden," Mrs. Connor added, "but you know your mother. They have season tickets to the Pops, so that's where they'll be. It's never the same without them. We'd love for you to come, though, and then you can take the credit for this lovely wall."

"*And* drum up mah business!" Mr. Connor added with a smile.

"I'll definitely try," Linden answered, thinking that maybe he would this year.

Mr. Connor helped him load his tools in his truck, and Mrs. Connor put the plate of freshly baked chocolate chip cookies on his passenger seat. Linden thanked them both and waved as he shifted gears. He looked in his rearview mirror and, watching them walk slowly back to their house, thought of all the good times he'd had there. It had practically been his second home when he was in high school.

When he reached the end of the driveway, he hesitated, and then turned right to head up the dirt road. Clouds of dust billowed behind the truck as he drove. A short distance away, at an old cedar post marking the northern boundary of the Connor property, he pulled over and gazed out the window. Finally, he got out and started to walk down the once familiar path. He looked around, amazed to find it unchanged. The stone cairn they'd built years ago was still standing; in fact, it even looked as if more stones had been added. Other than that, the rock outcropping was untouched, and seemingly eternal, in spite of his absence.

A gentle breeze cooled Linden's face and whispered of days gone by. He looked out across the valley and thought of the countless summer nights under the stars, the chilly autumn evenings after cross-country meets when they'd built a fire, and the sweet spring midnights after dances. Somehow they'd always ended up here, passing around a bottle of Boone's Farm or some other intoxicant, talking, laughing, and gazing at the stars, and never imagining their carefree days would end. Back then, with his arm around Callie, the future had seemed so certain, so full of hope. He wondered if the initials he'd scratched into one of the rocks were still visible or if time and the weather had worn them away. He climbed up and, with a sad smile, lightly traced his finger over the letters: L.F. + C.W. Then he leaned back against the rocks, felt their warmth, and remembered the last time he'd stood there.

It was the summer after Callie's mom died. They had not seen each other in several months, but they'd talked often on the phone, making plans for the summer that stretched ahead of them with only one more year apart. Then, out of the blue, Callie had called to say she was staying on campus for the summer, that she'd found a job. Yes, she'd come home for the Fourth, but she'd have to head right back. It was late when she'd finally arrived at the Connors' party. He had watched from a distance as she had greeted their friends but, when she'd come to him, she'd avoided looking in his eyes, and her hug had seemed stiff and forced. Dismayed, he had held her hands and asked her what was wrong, but she had just pulled away and said, "Nothing."

Later in the evening, he had asked her to go for a walk, and although she initially put him off, she'd finally agreed. They had walked down the road and sat on the rocks to watch the fireworks, but she had still seemed to be worlds away. Silently, they'd listened to the voices at the party, oohing and ahhing, and then the sky had filled with the brilliant lights of the finale and he had realized, in alarm, that tears were streaming down her cheeks. Bewildered, he'd pulled her up to face him, and pleaded, "Callie, tell me what's wrong."

She had turned away from him and stammered, "I . . . I don't think we should see each other anymore."

Linden looked up at the endless blue sky, crossed his arms tightly over his chest, and shook his head in dismay. *Why does it still hurt so much?*

5

The hospital wasn't far from the nursing home, but Henry was not happy about getting back in the hot car. Callie finally calmed him down with the promise that Papa was waiting.

"You can see him," the nurse said when they finally found his room, "but try not to wake him. He needs his rest." Callie nodded, clenching her jaw as she turned to go into her father's darkened room. A single shaft of afternoon sun filtered in through the drawn curtains. The only other light came from the machine blinking steadily beside his bed and tracking the blessed beats of his weary heart. She set Henry down, and he immediately walked over and stood in front of the machine to watch the pattern of lights. Callie pulled a chair quietly up to the bed. Her heart ached at the sight of so many tubes and wires crisscrossing the frail frame of the man who'd once held her in his strong arms.

"Oh, Dad," she whispered. *Where is that amazing man that danced me around the living room on his shoes, crooning an old Eddy Arnold song?* She could still hear his smooth tenor voice singing the melancholy lyrics about a world made for two. Callie closed her eyes and tried to remember the warm comfort of being held in his arms. She blinked back tears. *Where is that invincible man that always shouted from the sideline, "Go get 'em, kiddo! You can beat her!"*? She reached out and slipped her hand into his and, to her surprise, he gently squeezed. Callie looked up and he opened his eyes and whispered, "Don't worry, kiddo, everything'll be okay."

Callie wrapped her fingers around his calloused hand just as she had when she was a little girl sitting beside him in church. Back then, she'd whiled away the sermon studying every scar and callus and repeatedly tracing her fingers over his mountain range of knuckles, pausing on each one to whisper the name of one of the peaks in the Presidential Range.

"Oh, Dad," Callie whispered, "I'm so sorry I wasn't here."

"It's okay, honey," he murmured, opening his eyes and trying to look around. "Did you bring my handsome grandson with you?"

Callie nodded. "He's right here, Dad, entranced by your illuminated heartbeat."

"How is he?"

"He's fine." She paused, trying to decide if she should tell him.

"What did the doctor say?"

She continued holding his hand. "She said he might outgrow it." She paused, not wanting to upset him, but then continued quietly. "She said it's called autism and it's more commonly seen in boys. Symptoms can range from mild to severe, but she thinks Henry is on the low end of the 'spectrum'—that's what she called it. She also said it's something like a sensory overload."

Ben Wyeth nodded and closed his eyes, and Callie sat quietly with him for as long as Henry's mood would allow. Before they left she put the Bible on his bedside table, kissed him lightly on the cheek, and whispered they'd be back soon. He opened his eyes and smiled.

When they pulled into the driveway, Callie realized she'd been so lost in thought that she'd forgotten to stop at the store and she'd forgotten to ask her dad if she could borrow some money. She opened the fridge, wondering what she might find. On the top shelf was a half gallon of milk, a quart of orange juice, a jar of pickles, a bottle of Heinz ketchup, and a faded box of Arm & Hammer baking soda that looked like it had been there since the beginning of time. She shook her head in dismay. Not daring to smell the milk, she turned her head and listened to it plop into the sink. Then she turned on the faucet and dumped the orange juice too. She rinsed out both containers and threw them in the garbage. The fridge door had swung shut, as it always had after her dad, tired of it being left open, purposely made the front of the fridge higher than the back. Callie pulled open the door again and stuck out her knee to keep it open. On the shelf in the door was a sticky jar of grape jelly and, beside it, a jar missing its label but looking like marmalade. She opened the jelly jar and peered inside looking for evidence of a "science experiment"—a term her dad had liked to use for fuzzy growth on forgotten food. To her surprise, the only color she saw was purple, and the peanut butter she found in the cabinet hadn't even been opened yet. She still needed to go back out to the store, though, and pick up bread and milk and what little else her last five dollars would buy.

6

Linden sat on the tailgate of his truck in the hazy morning sun, studying the worn tread of his racers. He knew they would get him through the annual Firecracker 5K, but if he ever started running again he would definitely need to invest in some new shoes. He'd been wearing the same pair since high school and, over the years, they'd molded to his feet. At one time he'd considered having them resoled, but then he decided that no cobbler could ever replicate the classic Bowerman tread unless, of course, he used a hot waffle iron. He'd also considered sending the shoes back to Nike for resoling, but then he'd imagined the amused look on the face of the service agent who received them and speculated on the chances of having the same shoes returned to him. Nike would probably just send him their latest model with a note of regret. He had pictured his old shoes carelessly discarded in a garbage can and decided it was too risky.

He loosened his laces, slipped on his shoes, and gingerly pulled the laces tight, praying they wouldn't break. Then he dropped off the tailgate, stretched, and thought about the previous year's race. He'd traversed the rolling three-mile course with his former high school cross-country coach and English teacher, Asa Coleman. Mr. Coleman also owned the cabin where Linden lived, and in lieu of rent, Linden maintained the property for him and took care of any small carpentry jobs that arose.

His presence at the cabin also discouraged teenagers and rabble-rousers from breaking in and having parties and starting fires in the stone fireplace, an occurrence that had happened regularly when the cabin was unoccupied. Now Linden hoped to see his former coach again so he could talk to him about a couple of housekeeping projects that needed attention. He turned to lift the tailgate and saw Jon Connor trotting toward him. "Well, well, if it isn't the legendary Linden Finch!" Jon teased, stopping to shake hands. "How's it hangin'?"

Linden glanced inside the front of his shorts and shook his head in dismay. "Limp, as always."

Jon laughed. "That's what I've heard."

Linden smiled. "How've you been?"

"Fine, actually, *really* fine." Jon grinned. "I'm gettin' married."

"No!" Linden teased. "Who's the unfortunate soul?"

Jon laughed again. "She's back at the house. We got in last night—had to do the whole separate bedroom thing." He rolled his eyes. "By the way, my parents said you might grace us with your presence tonight."

Linden grinned. "I might."

"Well, you definitely should. Then you can meet her." Jon paused. "By the way, nice job on the wall."

"Thanks."

"So, are you showing off today or just out for fun? I can't keep up if you're showing off again."

Linden laughed and turned toward town. "Nope, just out for fun."

Jon fell into step beside him, caught sight of his old running shoes, and shook his head in dismay. "Please tell me you aren't still wearing those tired old Prefontaine racers? Don't you think it's time to break down and invest in some new shoes?"

"It's crossed my mind," Linden answered with a glance down at Jon's pristine New Balance trainers.

Runners were already lining up when they turned the corner onto Main Street, and although Linden saw several old teammates, there was no sign of his former teacher and coach. Moments later, the cannon boomed and Linden started his watch. He and Jon started off at an easy pace, but when runners started to pass them, Linden patted Jon on the back and said, "See you at the finish!" He pulled away, picking up his pace considerably.

A short time later, he crossed the finish line and glanced at his watch. *Not bad for no training,* he thought, *but not even close to my best. Those days are long gone.* He looked around to see if Jon had come in yet, but there was no sign of him. He waited, watching the now-steady stream of runners.

"Hey, Linden! How'd you do?"

Linden turned and smiled. "Under 17. How 'bout you?"

"Just came in," Mr. Coleman answered, smiling and catching his breath. "These old muscles just don't fire like they used to." Linden nodded, and as they walked around together, he took the opportunity to mention the repairs at the cabin.

"Two of the porch steps need some attention and one of the back window frames is rotting."

Mr. Coleman nodded. "No problem. Whatever needs doing—just charge the materials to my account."

Linden nodded, and his former teacher eyed him. "I mean it."

"I know you *mean* it," Linden replied with a grin.

Another runner joined them, and Mr. Coleman

took the water he offered. He paused thoughtfully, looking from one to the other. "Linden, you remember my son Noah." It was more of a statement than a question.

Linden nodded and reached out to shake hands. "It's been a while," he said. Although Noah was much older, Linden remembered seeing him at cross-country meets. In fact, Noah was a bit of a legend among the high school runners because he still held several unchallenged records.

Linden looked from Noah to Mr. Coleman and realized he'd never seen them standing side by side. They looked more like brothers than father and son. Linden talked with them for a few minutes more and then wished them well and turned to go. As he walked away, a slender, blond-haired boy ran by, and Linden glanced over his shoulder and watched him stop breathlessly in front of Mr. Coleman and Noah.

"Hey, Dad, Grampa," he exclaimed, "I did it! I broke 18!"

Linden drove slowly past the tidy little ranch that sat back from the road. Mr. Wyeth's old pickup was parked in the driveway, and beside it, under a leaning, rusty basketball hoop, was the Chevy Nova that Callie had driven in high school. The screen door was wide open, but there didn't seem to be anyone around. Linden suddenly wondered what he would do if Callie *was* around—if she just happened to be standing in the driveway. Would he quickly look away and pretend he didn't see her? Would he smile and wave? Would he stop? And if he stopped, what would he say? What *do* you say, after your heart has been broken, to the one who broke it? Do you just say, "Hi, how are you?" Do you act nonchalant as if nothing ever happened, as if all that you shared never really mattered? Or do you search that person's eyes, trying to understand, and then blurt out the only question you ever wanted to ask: *Do you realize what you did to me?*

Linden turned the truck toward home and wondered why he continued to torment himself. Why was he even thinking about Callie? And why the hell, after all these years, couldn't he move on?

7

Callie glanced at the calendar hanging on the wall above her dad's desk. It was still turned to January, and a dilapidated Plymouth, abandoned in a snowy Vermont field, graced the scene. She took the calendar down, turned it to July, and looked at the picture of a forgotten Chevy Nomad with a tree growing up where the engine had once been. She looked at the date: Sunday, July 4, 1999. If her mom were alive, holiday or not, they'd be getting ready for church. She hung the calendar up, broke down the last empty box, and dropped it on top of the others on the bed in the spare room. Henry had fallen asleep on the couch the night before, right after they'd had scrambled eggs and toast for supper. Callie had carried him down the hall and gently laid him on the bed, and then she'd spent the rest of the evening unpacking. That morning, while he was busy playing with his LEGOs, she'd finished unpacking his toys and finally decided to leave her boxes of kitchenware stacked in the garage. *Who knows when I will need them again.*

She lifted a flattened pile of boxes and maneuvered them clumsily down the narrow hall that divided the cozy, modest ranch down its middle. "Ready for lunch?" she called as she passed the living room, but then stopped in her tracks. Colorful towers of LEGOs were arranged in neat rows on the carpet, but Henry was not there.

"Hen-Ben?" Callie dropped the boxes on the table and hurried back down the hall. She quickly scanned the bedrooms and then went back to look under each of the beds and in the closets. "Henry?" she called as she pulled back the shower curtain. "Henry, where are you?" Her heart and mind began to race. *Oh, God, where is he? Please let me see him!*

She ran into the kitchen and down the stairs to the basement. Her voice was strained. "Henry, are you hiding on me?" But there was no sign of him anywhere. Callie flew back up the stairs and realized the screen door was open. She clearly remembered clicking the little metal lever down and pushing on the door to make sure it held. But now it wasn't even latched, and the breeze blew it open and closed. "Henry, where are you?" she shouted.

She pushed open the door and shouted his name. She looked in the garage, her car, her dad's truck, all around the house, and then she ran down the driveway to the road, but there was still no sign of him. She was absolutely beside herself as she hurried down the road. She stopped at the intersection with the town road and then backtracked past her parents' house and up the hill, feeling as if she had been swept into a terrible dream. She kept picturing the way Henry furrowed his brow fretfully when he was concentrating . . . and then she was overwhelmed by the terrifying thought that she would never see that look again. A sickening wave of nausea swept over her. "Oh, God, please let me find him," she pleaded. "I'll do anything. Just let me find him." She looked up at the sky and begged, "Please, if you just show me where he is, I promise I'll never ask you for anything ever again." She paused to listen, certain that God would answer such a selfless prayer, but all she heard were songbirds, chirping and fluttering in

47

the bushes, their seemingly cheerful indifference only adding to her agony. Finally, she pulled herself up, clenched her fists, and loudly commanded, "Henry! Answer me!"

8

Linden was still in a bit of a funk when he pulled into the yard. Kat and Springer were happily oblivious to his mood, though, and greeted him with sloppy tennis balls entrenched in their mouths. At first, Linden shook his head. "Not now." But the dogs persisted, following him around and dropping their soggy treasures at his feet. Finally, he relented, picked up both balls, and threw them as far as he could. The dogs raced away and returned moments later, happily wagging their tails and nudging their tennis balls toward his feet. Linden continued to throw the balls until the dogs' tongues were dragging on the ground. "Okay, that's enough," he said, turning on the hose. Kat wagged her tail and slurped and snorted at the cold stream while Springer danced around, barking and chomping at it. Linden turned off the water and headed around the corner of the cabin. The dogs stood still, watching curiously, and then rounded up their tennis balls and bounded after him, grinning from ear to floppy ear. As they neared the river, the dogs plunged headfirst into the cold water, and Linden, laughing at their unabashed enthusiasm, pulled off his shirt, and joined them.

A while later he emerged, refreshed, from a deep swimming hole and sloshed up through the shallow current, looking down into the clear water as it rushed playfully over the smooth stones sparkling in the afternoon sun. Linden shook the beads of water from his hair, reached into a small pool lined with river rocks, and pulled the last icy bottle out from its depths; he also made a mental note that the natural cooler needed restocking *again*.

All of the riverbank amenities were already in place when Linden moved in: a fire pit with a small stack of seasoned wood, two weathered Adirondack chairs, a rusty bottle opener hanging from a nail under the arm of one of the chairs, and a welcoming six-pack chilling in the river. Linden had replenished the supply of beer more times than he could count.

He opened the bottle, took a long drink, and studied the large pile of stones in the middle of the river. He stepped back into the water and walked out to it. He set his bottle on a nearby rock and, with the clear, cold water swirling around his calves, began gathering large, smooth stones from the river bottom and placing them one on top of one another on the pile. As the afternoon slipped by, a massive stone cairn rose from the river, and the laughing, carefree current swirled and rippled around the man-made obstacle, searching for a new course to follow. The lyrics of an old hymn ran through Linden's mind as he worked. *"Here I raise mine Ebenezer; hither by thy help I'm come; and I hope, by thy good pleasure, safely to arrive at home."*

9

"Henry!" Callie called frantically as she ran through the woods. Her shirt was torn and spattered with mud, and her arms and legs were covered with scratches from the unforgiving briars that ripped at her skin. "Oh, Henry, where are you?" she shouted as she retraced her steps toward the road. She knew she needed help; she should go back to the house and call for help, but then she remembered the phone was still out of order. She hurried on until she finally reached the dirt road again and looked toward the house. *Maybe he went back.* Then she looked up the hill. *Maybe he's just over the hill. If I go a little farther, maybe he's there.* She pushed herself to climb to the top of the grade, and then, she stared in disbelief. A small figure was running down the old woods road.

"Henry!" Callie cried. The figure stopped, looked up, and then continued to run. Callie raced down the hill, almost tripping several times before finally scooping him into her arms. She collapsed in an exhausted heap in the middle of the dirt road with thankful tears spilling down her cheeks. She buried her face in his sun-swept hair and breathed in his musky little boy scent mixed with the sweet scent of Johnson's baby shampoo. Innocently unaware, Henry just sat on her lap and lightly traced his finger over the dried blood and scratches that crisscrossed her arms and legs.

When they got back to the house, Callie set him on the counter in the bathroom, washed his face and arms with a cool washcloth, gave him another long hug, and finally let him go. She watched him wander into the living room, completely unaware of the trauma he'd caused. She latched the door again. In the morning, the first thing they'd be doing would be going to Belletetes for eyehooks. It was obvious that telling Henry not to leave the house was not enough. In fact, if the hardware store weren't closed for the holiday, they'd already be on their way.

That night, Callie made scrambled eggs and toast for supper again. She was thankful Henry wasn't a fussy eater. By the time she'd cleaned up the kitchen, given him a quick bath, and helped him into his pajamas, the sun was slipping from the summer sky. She had wanted to visit her dad that day, but they'd never gotten the chance. It was still light enough, though, to nestle together on the back porch and read one of Henry's favorite books. She'd found *Goodnight Moon* in a moving box full of towels but still had no idea how it had gotten there. They had read the little book so many times in the last two years that she didn't even need to look at the words anymore; she knew them all by heart. And Henry, for his part, never tired of hearing the story; he just waited for the pages to be turned so he could point triumphantly at the little mouse. Sometimes, Callie even thought she saw him smiling. For Henry, it was a new story and an old friend every time.

She lifted him up onto her lap, opened the book, and began, but her words were immediately interrupted by a popping sound somewhere in the distance. Henry looked up, frowning, and pointed. "It's nothing," Callie assured him, "just fire-crackers." She turned back to the book, but she was interrupted again. This time, she looked up at the sky and wondered if the Connors were having their Fourth of July party. She quickly pushed the thought away, wrapped her arms around Henry, and tried to refocus on the book, and the life she'd chosen.

10

Linden came in from doing chores, grabbed a cold Molson from the fridge, and headed straight for the shower. He turned on the water, glanced at the clock, and wondered how it had gotten so late.

He washed quickly and then leaned back and let the water drench his head and cool his sunburned shoulders. He thought about the day and wondered why he couldn't seem to get Callie off his mind; it was almost as if the possibility that she had come home had released a floodgate of memories. As the water rinsed the soap away, he closed his eyes and thought back to a hazy summer evening, years earlier, when Callie had stopped by on her way home from work.

She had been sandy and sunburned from lifeguarding all day, and her hair had seemed to have a mind of its own in the humidity. She'd leaned against her Nova, watching him wash his truck while they talked about what they should do that night. She'd said she just wanted to go home and take a shower, and Linden had held up the hose and teased, "Take off your suit." She'd rolled her eyes and he'd grinned. "Seriously, you *could* just shower here."

"Hmmm . . . I'm sure your parents would love that."

"They're in Boston."

"I know, silly, but don't you think they'd frown on me taking a shower when *you* are the only one home?"

Linden had turned off the hose and stood in front of her. "Why?" he'd teased. "What could happen?"

"Well, for starters, their seemingly innocent son might try to seduce his girlfriend . . . *again!*"

"Hmmm, has he done that before?" he'd murmured, kissing her neck.

Callie had leaned back against the car and closed her eyes. "Well, not successfully," she'd said softly. "But you know that old saying, 'If at first . . .'"

"I think I know the one," he'd whispered, slipping his hands under her shirt onto the silky, taut material of her bathing suit. His hands had glided smoothly up along the curve of her body. "Hmmm," he'd teased, "what's goin' on here?"

"I wonder," she'd replied. "Maybe the same thing that's goin' on down here," she'd whispered, pressing against him.

Linden opened his eyes and sipped his beer. It was late and he needed to get going, but the memory of Callie's body pressed against him had aroused more than his mind. He closed his eyes, leaned back, and let the water rush over his body.

An hour later, Linden parked his truck out on the road and walked toward the Connors' brightly lit house. He could hear laughter coming from the backyard and splashing from the pool. He hesitated, wondering if it was too late to turn around and head home. But as he stood in the driveway, considering, a familiar voice called mockingly, "Well, well, can it be?" and Linden knew it was already too late. He peered into the shadows, trying to make out a face, but all he could see was the orange glow of a cigarette. As

54

he drew closer, a fragrant cloud drifted from the garage, and he realized it wasn't a cigarette.

Josh Connor stepped to the edge of the light, wearing a faded black Grateful Dead T-shirt, holding his breath, and grinning sheepishly. He held out his joint, but Linden just held up his hand and shook his head.

"You'll never change, will you, Josh?" he surmised with a wry smile.

Josh shrugged his shoulders, exhaled slowly, and sputtered, "Why change?" The two former classmates shook hands, and Josh pulled a bottle of Coors from a nearby cooler, twisted off the top, and handed it to Linden. While they were talking, two girls came around the corner of the garage, giggling and sipping a concoction that smelled strongly of tequila. They were both tan, barefoot, and wearing very short cutoffs and bikini tops.

"Hey, Josh," the slender redhead scolded, "I thought you were goin' to share . . ." She stopped and smiled politely when she saw that there was someone in the garage with her brother and then she realized who it was. "Oh, my God! Linden! You came!" She hugged him with such unabashed enthusiasm that she accidently spilled her drink. "I can't believe it!" she exclaimed. Linden just smiled; *he* couldn't believe how grown-up Katie had become.

"C'mon," she said as she slipped her hand into

Linden's and pulled him toward the door. "Come say hi to my parents." Katie's friend, however, opted to hang out in the shadows with Josh, claiming she just loved Billy Joel and wanted to listen to "I've Loved These Days," which was playing on the radio.

"She *really* just loves Josh," Katie confided in a whisper, "*and* getting high!"

Mr. Connor was flipping burgers when they came around the corner of the house. "Well, well, here's the mastah wahl buildah!" he exclaimed happily. "Hope yah brought your appahtite!"

Mrs. Connor gave Linden a warm hug and then proceeded to heap macaroni salad, potato salad, Jell-O salad, two deviled eggs, and baked beans on a plate for him so that, by the time Mr. Connor offered him a cheeseburger, there was no room for it. Linden made a gallant effort, though, and tucked his beer bottle against his chest so he could balance the full plate in one hand and take the cheeseburger in the other. He smiled helplessly at Katie, and she immediately saw his dilemma. Laughing, she took the beer from under his arm, put it on the table, and pulled out a chair for him. Then she went to ask Jon if he would make a fresh margarita for her. Linden watched her go and saw Jon eyeing her suspiciously. From Katie's gestures he could tell she was having trouble convincing him that she had really spilled her drink. Jon looked at Linden, held up Katie's cup,

56

and pointed at it with raised eyebrows. Linden wasn't sure if he was asking for confirmation that she was telling the truth or asking him if he wanted one too, so he just shook his head and pointed to his beer. Jon nodded and retreated into the house while Katie came back over to the table, rolling her eyes. "I don't know why he doesn't believe me!"

"Have you eaten?" Linden asked, swallowing a deviled egg in one gulp.

"I've been picking," she replied.

"Well, if you're gonna drink that evil stuff, you should eat."

She eyed him. "What, do I have three big brothers now?"

Linden smiled. "You always have."

Katie grinned mischievously. "But I've *always* wanted so much more!"

"Hmmm," he replied, studying her eyes. "How much *have* you had?"

"Not enough," she said, laughing and reaching to take the replenished cup her brother was holding out.

Jon pulled up another chair and motioned to a pretty brunette who was standing by the pool. She walked over and Jon introduced her. "Linden, I'd like you to meet my fiancée, Julie."

Linden stood to shake hands. "It's nice to meet you," he said. He paused thoughtfully and then teased, "I don't know if I should say congratulations or good luck!" Julie laughed good-naturedly and sat down in the chair next to Jon, and he slid his cup to her.

He turned back to Linden. "So, what was your time this morning?"

"Under 17," Linden said with a slow smile.

"I thought you weren't showing off."

"I wasn't," Linden replied, bringing his beer to his lips and winking at Katie.

"You shouldn't do that," she said flirtatiously. "I might get ideas."

Linden looked at Jon and shook his head. "I think you better cut her off."

Katie leaned back, took a sip, and grinned at them.

I I

"Time for bed," Callie whispered softly. Henry squirmed away from her and made a move toward the porch steps. "Oh, no, you don't!" she said, standing to catch him. But just as he reached the top step, the distant sky filled with sparkling bright lights. Henry came to an abrupt halt and pointed. "Fireworks," Callie said. "Do you want to go see them?" Henry just stared into the darkness. "Stay there," she said, eyeing him. "I'll be right out." She went into the kitchen, grabbed Henry's sweatshirt and her keys, and closed the door. She knew the best place from which to watch the fireworks was up at the rocks, and she hoped no one would be there.

They bumped up the dirt road, and Callie turned the car around and parked on the opposite side, headed down. She lifted Henry out and helped him pull his sweatshirt on over his pajamas. He was wide-eyed as she picked him up and carried him down the path shrouded in darkness. When they reached the lookout, she sat down on the rocks with him on her lap and tried *not* to think about the last time she'd sat there.

They didn't have to wait long before sparks flew into the air and disappeared, seemingly without fanfare. A moment later, though, the sky exploded into a cascade of brilliant lights raining down, and these were soon followed by several thundering detonations that echoed across the valley.

Henry squirmed and whimpered, and Callie hugged him. "It's okay, Hen-Ben," she assured him. "There's nothing to be afraid of; it's just lights and sounds." As she said this, though, a succession of small rockets screamed into the darkness and exploded into swirling, confusing lights . . . and these were followed by more deafening detonations. Henry cried out and frantically tried to cover his eyes and ears. Callie suddenly remembered the doctor's words and realized that Henry wasn't afraid. He was in pain, and not just any pain. *The doctor had said it could be excruciating pain!*

"I'm sorry, Hen-Ben!" Callie said remorsefully, holding on to his thrashing, twisting body and trying *not* to get hit by the small fists that were fiercely clapping on the sides of his head. "I'm sorry, I wasn't thinking! I wasn't thinking! Let's go! Let's go home!" She tried desperately to calm him, but the relentless assault on his senses seemed to be unbearable. She held him close to her body and tried to shelter his head with her arms as she stumbled back up the path.

12

Linden was surveying the dessert table when Katie came up behind him and whispered, "Nice ass!"

Linden picked up a homemade brownie and raised his eyebrows. "Is that how you talk to all your brothers?" he teased. Katie just rolled her eyes.

Mr. Connor looked up and realized the outdoor lights were still on, spied Linden standing near the door, and hollered to him. Linden went inside and found the switch, but when he reemerged into the dark yard, he thought he heard an odd sound. He stood still, trying to listen over the noise of the party and, after the second burst of fireworks, he heard it again. Puzzled, he walked slowly around the house and up the driveway. By the time he reached the road, he had realized that it was a child crying. With his heart pounding, he started to run. *Why is there a child out here?* he wondered. As he drew closer, the cries grew louder but, just as he reached the top of the last knoll, they were suddenly drowned out by the sound of a loud engine sputtering to life and he could only watch helplessly as the taillights of an old car flickered down the road.

"Where'd you go?" Katie asked when he walked back down the driveway. "You missed the fireworks."

"I thought I heard something," he replied, still puzzled.

"And . . ."

He shrugged and shook his head. "I don't know."

Katie leaned against one of the cars and almost lost her balance. "I think you've had enough," Jon surmised, "*and* I think you're going to be sorry tomorrow. Haven't you learned anything about moderation at that Ivy League school?"

Katie scowled at him and sneered, "More than you!"

Josh agreed. "Hey, Jon, give her a break. I can remember several times at Brown when you could be found worshipping the porcelain goddess. Let's see, tequila shots in the dorm followed by White Russians at Spats? You were three sheets to the wind! And the next day you couldn't even run at the invite."

Katie folded her arms across her chest and smirked at her brother. "Gee, I never heard that one before."

"Thanks, Josh," Jon said, putting his arm around Julie. "That was a family secret."

"Hey!" Katie protested indignantly. "*I'm* family!"

"Sorry to break it to you," Jon teased callously, "but *you* were adopted, hence the red hair and freckles. Didn't you notice? No one else in the family has them."

"Thasnot true!" Katie began to slur her words. "Mom said Aunt Ruth did." She glanced at Linden, who was standing by himself, innocently observing the sibling discord, but when he inadvertently smiled, she drunkenly turned the tables. "At least I'm not foolish enough to believe that someone would just stop going out with me for no reason."

Jon winced at his sister's words. "Katie, what does that have to do with anything?"

She looked at him. "Well, it's true and you know it! Everyone in town knows it!" Katie's tone had all of a sudden become accusatory and sharp. "Maybe it's time Linden learned the truth. Maybe it's time one of his *real* friends told him the *real* reason Callie broke up with him."

Josh stepped up beside Katie and put his arm around her. "I think it's time for all unruly children to go to bed." He tried to guide Katie toward the house, but she twisted away from him, swaying precariously, and refocused on Linden. Jon stepped toward her too, but she pushed him away and almost fell again.

A small group had begun to gather in the driveway and Katie felt encouraged by their interest. She took a sip from her cup and announced matter-of-factly, "Callie was pregnant, Linden. That's why she broke up with you." She swayed a bit before continuing. "The father of the baby is a big mystery too, but I heard he was married."

Linden, who had been curiously waiting to hear what she was going to say, just stared at her.

"Katie, shut up, okay? You've said enough!" Jon commanded.

"But, thersmore, Jon," she slurred, leaning on the car to steady herself. "I heard something's wrong with him. I heard her son's retarded and thaswhyshestocome home."

Josh whistled softly. "Nice, Katie, you certainly have a way with words."

Katie looked at her brother defiantly. "He was going to find out anyway. Don't you think it's better that he find out from us?"

"You mean from you," Jon corrected.

Linden didn't say a word. He just listened to them talk about him as if he weren't there, and then he bit his lip and looked away. Finally, he turned and started to walk toward his truck. Jon called after him. "Linden, wait. . . ."

But Linden just put up his hand and said, "Thank your parents for me."

Twenty minutes later, Linden was sitting on the dark porch with the dogs, watching the stars flicker and fade and then grow bright again. Katie's words echoed through his head and, for the first time in a long time, Linden thought about the months that had followed his breakup with Callie.

After that Fourth of July, he had been devastated and confused, and he'd had no desire to return to school. His parents had argued vehemently with him about making such a rash decision and he'd answered them by drinking his way through the summer and fall months, trying desperately to forget. By Christmas, he'd had all he could take of his mother's constant badgering, and he packed up his things, brushed the snow off his truck, emptied his savings account, and headed south. He had no plan. He just wanted to get away from everyone— and everything—that reminded him of Callie. With no particular destination in mind, he just drove, sleeping in truck stops, eating in diners, and continuing on until he reached Georgia.

He had pulled into a quiet parking lot to take a nap, not at all sure of where he was. But when he woke up, he realized he had parked right in front of a sign marking the beginning of the Appalachian Trail. Initially surprised by its appearance on his wayward path, he had had a sudden epiphany: *What better way to numb emotional torment than with physical suffering?* He'd climbed out of the truck, stood in front of the sign, and thought about the countless backpacking trips he'd been on as a Boy Scout. In fact, he'd probably already hiked the hardest parts of the Appalachian Trail—through the White Mountains. At that moment, he decided, and, by mid-February, he had sold his truck, bought a used backpack, and researched the supplies he'd need to thru-hike the entire trail. In the weeks that followed, he bought a tent, rain gear, nonperishable food, and a lightweight cooking set. His final purchase was a pair of leather hiking boots, which he promptly trudged through puddles and mud to break in.

Then, on a cold, rainy March morning he dropped a picture postcard of the Chattahoochee National Forest addressed to his parents into a mailbox outside the courthouse in Dahlonega, Georgia; hitched his backpack onto his shoulders; pulled the straps tight; and turned toward Springer Mountain. He signed into the AT log book under the trail name Wounded Finch and disappeared into the wild terrain of the most famous footpath on the East Coast. No one heard from him again until he emerged at the summit of Mount Katahdin five months later with a full beard and two dogs by his side.

But still, in the years that followed that trip, how was it that he'd never heard about Callie? Especially if, as Katie said, everyone knew. His parents had surely found out before they'd moved back to Boston, and his mother would have certainly told him. It would have been a major coup for her in her effort to prove that Callie wasn't the right girl for him. Linden just couldn't believe she would have been able to withhold such damning evidence.

But all this was beside the point because, if it was true, then how . . . and why? Oh, Callie, why?

13

Callie silently berated herself while Henry cried inconsolably in the backseat. *How can I be so stupid? What was I thinking? I wasn't, obviously! What kind of mother does this to her child?* When they finally got home again, she lifted him out and whispered, "I'm sorry, Hen-Ben. It's obviously going to take me a while to figure this out, but I will, I will! I promise!" She sat him on the bathroom counter, pulled off his sweatshirt, gently wiped his face with a warm washcloth, and helped him get ready for bed. She pulled down the Mickey Mouse sheets and Henry, finally calm and rubbing his eyes, pointed to Mickey and climbed in. He also pointed to Travelin' Bear, and Callie handed him the beloved brown bear. Henry tucked him under his chest, and Callie knelt beside him and gently pushed the wisps of blond hair back from his forehead. Then she closed her eyes and whispered his prayer. When she opened them again, he was sound asleep.

She got up and got ready for bed too, and then fell onto the bed in the next room. Even though she knew Henry was exhausted and would probably sleep through the night, she couldn't stop worrying. Every time she dozed off, she dreamed he was running down the road and she'd wake up with a pounding heart. Finally, she just got up, pulled her old patchwork sleeping bag out of her closet, and lay down on the floor next to his bed. She finally slept, but the next morning when she got up to make coffee, every muscle in her body ached.

She reached for the coffee can and thought about all the things she wanted to do that morning: the hardware store, food shopping, and visiting her dad, all before lunch, all before Henry grew tired, and all before the phone company came to restore service. As she lifted the plastic top off the can, she suddenly pictured a similar can that her dad had always kept in the back of his closet. The only reason she knew about the can was because she had knocked it over once when she was playing hide-and-seek with a friend. But, in the years that followed that misstep, she'd sometimes peeked in the closet to check on its continued existence, but that was a long time ago, and now she didn't think it would still be there. She went down the hall and, feeling as oddly intrusive as she had back then, opened his closet door. The familiar scent of Aqua Velva drifted from his suits and, when she knelt under them, they felt as if they were cloaking her in protective warmth. She started to move an old wooden box to the side but then stopped, pulling the box toward her and opening it to look at its neatly stored contents. She remembered her dad opening the wooden box's hinged top and setting out the items he needed to polish his shoes: the small round can of black Kiwi shoe polish, the torn cotton rag covered with brown and black smudges, and the long, soft belt of chamois cloth. She could hear him whistling softly and could still see his hands as they worked: twisting the clever mechanism on the side of the can to pop off the top, dabbing just the right amount of soft, dark polish on his already-shiny shoes, rubbing it evenly into the smooth leather, and then stretching the chamois tight and tugging it swiftly back and forth across the top of his shoe until it shone. When he finished his shoes, he had always looked up at her and politely inquired, "Shoe shine, Miss?" And Callie had always responded with a shy nod, holding out her scuffed Mary Janes. Her father had set the box in front of her, and she'd placed her shoe on the shoe-shaped handle and he'd start the process all over. When he had come to the final shine, he had always folded the soft chamois in half the long way so he wouldn't get polish on her snow-white stockings, and then he'd tug it back and forth so fast that it tickled her toes and made her giggle. She had loved having her shoes shined.

Callie's thoughts were suddenly interrupted by the quiet stillness of the house and her heart stopped. *Where is Henry?* She hurried down the hall, looking in all the rooms, but to her relief, she found him in the bathroom, meticulously lining up the toiletries. She looked at his neat arrangement of creams, shampoos, perfumes, and Dixie cups and wondered if she would ever understand how his mind worked.

She returned to her dad's closet, pushed aside the garments, and couldn't believe her eyes. Lined up in the shadow along the back wall were eight dark blue coffee cans, overflowing with bills and coins.

14

On Monday morning, Linden was up and out early. He pulled around to the lumber yard behind Belletetes. He needed a twelve-foot length of fir to replace the rotting pine steps and two narrower widths of cedar for the window frame. He also needed stain, but he'd have to get that inside.

• • •

Callie parked in front of Belletetes and helped Henry climb out. She'd let him walk as long as he held her hand. All they needed were eyehooks, but if his mood allowed she also hoped to look at the gadgets that were used for child-proofing. She glanced down at him as he trundled along beside her. *Sometimes he can be so good!*

"Hey, Linden, what can I get for you?" Linden turned to see Jack Ryan walking toward him. They talked briefly and Linden told him about his projects. Jack picked out three perfect boards, straight and clear of knots, and Linden slid them into the bed of his truck. When Jack asked if there was anything else, Linden said he was all set with wood but needed to go inside and look at the stain. Jack nodded and handed him a slip for the wood. Linden thanked him and walked toward the back entrance of the store. It was still early, but he could already feel the oppressive summer heat radiating from the pavement.

Henry was wide-eyed as Callie guided him past the myriad of charcoal grills, shovels, wheel-barrows, wagons, and even a John Deere lawn tractor. Henry pulled toward the tractor, but Callie was firm. "Not now. Maybe on the way out if you're good." They made their way to an ancient set of wooden drawers in the back of the store that catalogued every size nut, bolt, and screw imaginable. Callie held on to Henry's hand as she tried to decipher the system and find the drawer containing eyehooks. Suddenly, Henry reached up and pulled out a drawer labeled ¾″ Lag. The old system of drawers, Callie quickly discovered, had no stops, and the one Henry pulled on slid all the way out and clattered loudly to the floor, scattering its contents across the worn linoleum. Surprised and frightened, Henry yanked his hand free from Callie's grasp and covered his ears. Distracted and embarrassed, Callie let go and knelt down to pick up the bolts, but when she looked up, Henry was gone.

Linden stood in front of the Cabot display and tried to remember the color he needed. He could see the stain-dripped can on the basement shelf, but he couldn't for the life of him remember the name of the color. He was studying the chart when he heard a loud crash in the back of the store. He winced and wondered what poor soul had caused the loud calamity. A moment later, quick, light footfalls drew close to his aisle. He looked up in time to see a little boy run past.

Callie had just slid the refilled drawer back into place when a teenage clerk appeared and asked her if she needed help. "I *do* need help! I was trying to find eyehooks," she said in a flustered voice. "But, right now, I need to find my son." She turned away from the perplexed clerk and hurried to find Henry. The clerk shrugged, walked over to an adjacent wall, lifted two packages containing different-sized hooks off a display rack, and called after her, "I'll just bring the hooks to the counter." Callie nodded and tried to remain calm. *I cannot panic every time I lose sight of him,* she thought. *Besides, how far can he get in a hardware store?* She thought of the tractor and headed in that direction, calling his name and looking up and down every aisle.

Linden finally decided he would have to wait on the stain. He hung the chart back up and started to walk toward the register to pay for the wood. As he neared the end of the aisle, the small running figure he'd seen a moment ago rounded the corner at full speed and plowed headlong into his legs. "Whoa, there, little fella! Where are you off to in such a hurry?" He picked the boy up and their eyes locked. Then Linden heard someone calling and felt the boy squirm. Linden studied his face. "Are *you* Henry?" he asked, poking his finger at Henry's chest and smiling. Linden heard the voice draw closer and made his way toward it. A young woman walked hurriedly down the next aisle and Linden called after her, "Excuse me, ma'am, is this who you're looking for?"

• • •

Callie stopped at the sound of the familiar voice but didn't turn around. Instead, she tried to think, not knowing what to expect, not ready for *this* moment. She unwittingly bit her lip as she tried to fight back the tears that were suddenly stinging her eyes. Finally, giving up, she turned and, through the blur of remorse, looked at the face of the boy . . . man . . . who was holding her son in his arms.

Linden's heart stopped. For years he had wondered what he would do—what he would say—at this moment. And now all he could *do* was clench his jaw, and all he could *say,* in a voice barely audible, was, "Hey . . ."

"Hey . . ." came her soft reply.

They stood silently on the edge of disbelief, trying to absorb each other's presence, trying to grasp each other's continued existence on Earth because, up until this moment, they had only been haunted by the memory of that existence and, up until that moment, all they had been doing were the things that were necessary to sustain life but not to actually *live* it.

"I'm sorry," Callie said, nodding toward Henry and reaching out to take him. "Thank you for corralling him."

"It's okay," Linden said, smiling at the little boy who, he realized now, looked just like his mother.

73

Henry had just lost interest in the button on Linden's faded blue oxford and begun to squirm. Linden stepped forward and handed him to Callie.

"How've *you* been?" she asked with a smile that stole his heart.

Linden searched Callie's eyes and his mind filled with a long litany of rehearsed replies. "Fine," he lied. "You?"

"Oh, managing," she said with a tired smile.

"How's your dad?"

"He's . . . he's in the hospital," she stammered.

"I'm sorry. What happened?"

Callie's chest tightened. "He had a stroke and . . ." Henry began to protest at the delay, and Callie shook her head in dismay. "I'd better go."

Linden nodded.

"It was good to see you."

"It was good to see you too."

Linden stood and watched in stunned silence as the only girl he'd ever loved turned and walked away with her little boy in her arms.

PART II

Ah, when to the heart of man
Was it ever less than a treason
To go with the drift of things,
To yield with a grace to reason

—Robert Frost

15

Callie's heart was still pounding when she reached her car. Henry had made a fuss when she'd tried to pry him from the tractor seat, and she could only pray that Linden had already left the store and hadn't heard the commotion or witnessed the humiliating scene of her son rolling on the floor. There was a fine line, she decided, between a child's inability to cope with his surroundings and just plain bad behavior. *Every child has tantrums,* she thought, *so how does the parent of a child with autism know if the trigger is some inner turmoil or plain, old-fashioned defiance?* She looked at Henry's teary eyes and wanted, more than anything, to understand. She slipped the toy tractor the store owner had given her into his hands, knowing full well that he'd just wanted them to leave. Henry wiped his eyes and studied the little John Deere. Callie was not a fan of bribery, but at the moment it was the only thing that seemed to work. Besides, with Henry, she believed giving him something new to play with could just as easily be characterized as distraction.

She opened the car door and the trapped heat rolled out. She threw her wallet and the bag of eyehooks onto the passenger seat and reached into her pocket for her keys. Her heart sank; her pockets were empty. She must have left them on the counter. She looked in the rearview mirror at Henry, who was already strapped in. She could not bring him back in the store and she couldn't leave him in the car. She rested her aching head on the steering wheel, felt beads of perspiration trickling down the sides of her face, and recalled all the horrible stories about people who left their children and pets in vehicles unattended in the summer heat. Finally, in frustration, she looked through the windshield and fumed, "Do you think you could let *one* thing go my way?"

She got back out of the car and marched around to Henry's door. Just as she did, a blue Ford pickup drove out of the lumber yard and slowed down beside her. Callie looked up, embarrassed, and Linden stopped and asked, "Is everything okay?" Callie explained her dilemma.

"Go get them," he said. "I'll stay here."

She looked at him in amazement. "Are you sure?"

Linden put the truck in park and said simply, "Go." Callie ran back inside and found her keys where she'd left them. When she came back out, Linden was standing beside the car with Henry's door open.

She gave him a relieved smile. "You don't know what a huge help that was."

Linden nodded and Callie studied him, still unable to believe that he was actually standing in front of her, handsome and honest, still wearing faded Levis that hung from his slender hips in the same easy way they always had . . . and still smiling that same sweet, sheepish smile. The years hadn't touched him. She watched him push his dark chestnut hair back with his long, tan piano player fingers, and she searched his eyes for a trace of the tender passion they'd once known.

Henry suddenly threw the tractor out on the pavement, and Linden reached down to pick it up. "Seems like you have your hands full," he said, handing the tractor to her. And then, without considering, added, "If you ever need anything, I'm living in Mr. Coleman's cabin down by the river."

Callie nodded, remembering their teacher's cabin. More than anything, she wished she could stay and talk, but Henry had started to kick the seat again.

Linden climbed into his truck and gripped the steering wheel tightly as he pulled away. In his rearview mirror he watched Callie give the tractor back to Henry. He didn't understand why her little boy had misbehaved in the store, but he did know, from the solemn look in his clear blue eyes, that Callie's son was *not,* as Katie had drunkenly and callously announced, "retarded."

Linden turned into the driveway and parked under the ancient oak trees that shaded the barn and most of the front yard. As soon as he opened his door, Springer, with little regard for sensitive body parts, launched clumsily into the cab and greeted him with wet, sloppy kisses. "Hop down, you big moose," Linden said, gently pushing him out of the truck. No matter what the dogs did, Linden never scolded them; he knew that if he raised his voice or even looked at them the wrong way, they'd be crushed. Besides, he also knew that if it weren't for their providential appearance on his hike through the woods, he would've had a much harder time pulling his life together.

He remembered an observation one fellow hiker had made in a trail logbook after Linden had told him about his new companions: *To Wounded Finch: Labs will love you with all their hearts and follow you to the ends of the earth,* especially *if you feed them!*" It was true. Linden had been sitting on a sunny rock in Damascus, Virginia, minding his own business and devouring a ham-and-cheese grinder when the first of two undernourished Labs had emerged from the woods with her nose in the air. Spying Linden, she'd immediately plopped down in front of him and, with sad brown eyes, followed every move of his hand as it carried food to his mouth. Reluctantly, he'd held out his last morsel and she'd taken it with gentle politeness. A moment later another Lab trundled out of the woods and plopped down beside her. By then, all Linden had left was an apple, but the dogs didn't mind; they were happy to share whatever he had.

Linden had spent the rest of that day and half of the next asking in town if anyone recognized the two wayward dogs, but no one did. The dogs didn't seem worried about their lack of a home. They just followed Linden around on his inquiry and then fell into step beside him when he finally resumed hiking.

In the days that followed, their playful antics had made the trail much more of an adventure than an endurance test, and at night, their presence brought comfort and warmth when they curled up on either side of him. As the weeks passed and they hiked into New England, Linden discovered that, even though his backpack was heavier with their extra food, his heart was much lighter.

He slid the new boards out of the back of the truck, set them down on the porch, and went inside to pour a cold glass of sweet tea. He thought of the stain and went to the basement to look at the can on the shelf; it was called Pacific Redwood. Then he came back upstairs and took his iced tea outside. The dogs followed him down to the river and splashed playfully while he settled into one of the chairs. He had plenty to do, but it could wait. He needed time to think.

16

Callie had no time to dwell on the events of that morning. She pulled into the shopping plaza and ran down her list in her head: *peanut butter, jelly, cereal, o.j., bread, spaghetti, sauce, lettuce, tomatoes, apples, blueberries, if they're on sale, muffins would be good . . . lemon for zest then . . . Bisquick for pancakes . . . was there syrup in the fridge? Why didn't I write all this down?* As she lifted Henry into the shopping cart, she silently prayed that she wouldn't run into anyone she knew and that Henry wouldn't have another meltdown. She pushed the cart through produce, picking out the fruits and veggies she needed, and then continued past the beer case. *When was the last time I relaxed enough to have a beer?*

Henry was still cooperating when they finally reached frozen food, and Callie, stopping in front of the ice-cream case, was surprised to see Vermont's Ben & Jerry's on New Hampshire shelves. She wondered if she should splurge. "What do you think, Hen-Ben, Cherry Garcia or their new flavor, Peanut Butter and Jelly?" Henry shook his head and began to slam his toy tractor against the cart handle, and Callie realized that her time was up. She hurried toward checkout, but when she reached the end of the aisle, her heart sank. There were only two lanes open and both had long lines snaking down the aisles. She scolded herself for not getting through the store more quickly.

As they stood in line, Callie contemplated her dilemma. A child *without* autism might not even be able to tolerate such a long wait, but for Henry there was the additional strain of too much activity, too much noise, and too many bright lights. Callie looked at her full cart and considered apologizing and leaving it, but they really needed the food.

Suddenly, Henry threw his tractor to the floor and began to scream. Everyone looked up and watched as Callie picked up the tractor and tried to soothe him, but it was no use. *Oh, God, help me,* she prayed. Two seconds later, a cashier in a red smock appeared and motioned for her to come to a new lane. Callie couldn't believe her good fortune, and everyone in the store seemed to breathe a sigh of relief. An older gentleman even handed his key ring to Henry, and he miraculously stopped fussing long enough for Callie to finish. When she tried to pry the keys from his hand, though, he erupted into another fierce tantrum. Struggling with her son and her emotions, Callie finally freed the keys from his tight fist, handed them back to the man, stammered a quick thank you, and fled the store. Humiliated and certain that everyone was watching, she didn't look back.

Fifteen minutes later, she parked in the shade of

the old gnarled apple tree in the yard and helped Henry climb out. She gave him a bag to carry and, with her own arms full, followed him to the door. As she fumbled with her keys, she looked up and realized there was a door tag hanging from the knob. She saw the logo of the phone company and felt her cheeks flush in frustration. She tore the tag from the knob, unlocked the door, and brought the groceries inside. Henry put his bag down on the floor, lined up its contents on the kitchen table, and wandered off to the living room. Meanwhile, Callie compared the time on the clock to the time on the tag and realized she'd missed the service call by ten minutes! She stared through the screen door and then kicked it, hard, cracking the wooden panel.

Callie! She could almost hear her father's voice. *Get a handle on your temper!* She stared out at his gardens. *I know, Dad. I'm sorry.* For the first time since she'd moved home, she noticed that the weeds in the garden were almost as tall as the flowers. *Don't worry, Dad. I'll take care of them.* With a sigh, she turned from the door and began to put the groceries away.

She held the fridge open with one knee while she put away the milk, eggs, blueberries, and orange juice, and then took out the grape jelly. When everything was where it belonged, she opened the bag of Wonder bread and, as she made sandwiches for Henry and herself, she recalled how much her dad loved white bread. His favorite had been from Cumberland Farms, and although Wonder bread had been a close second, Cumby's was definitely first. She took out two more slices and smoothed peanut butter on both of them. When she was growing up, her dad, a history teacher, had always been the one to make lunch because her mom, a nurse, had always left early. Peanut butter and jelly had been his specialty, and his secret trick was to spread peanut butter on both slices of bread so the jelly didn't soak into the bread and make it soggy. *The peanut butter acts as a sealer,* he'd say. Then he'd cut the sandwich in half, tear off a perfect size piece of wax paper, stack the two halves on top of one another to conserve wax paper *and* lunchbox space, and deftly wrap the sandwich with crisp, neat folds that she never learned to replicate. Callie looked in the drawer for the familiar blue-and-red box of Cut-Rite Wax Paper. She'd just have to give those folds another try.

"We're going to see Papa," she announced after lunch. Henry was busy arranging the chairs in a neat row again but immediately stopped and headed for the door when he heard the word "Papa."

17

"You guys are *not* coming in!" Linden said, closing the screen door behind him. He looked out at the two wet dogs wagging their tails hopefully. "Go find a sunny spot and maybe I'll bring out a treat." They wiggled harder when they heard their favorite word and then plopped down promptly, thinking he meant *now*. Linden shook his head and retreated to the kitchen to make a quick PB&J on soft wheat, which he ate over the sink and washed down with a tall glass of cold milk. When he'd finished he brushed the crumbs into the sink, rinsed his glass, and put it in the dish drain, wondering when the last time was that that glass had actually seen soap. *Oh, well, it doesn't matter. I'm the only one who drinks from it.*

Remembering the dogs, he lifted off the top of the ceramic canister on the counter and took out two dog biscuits. He quietly pushed on the screen door and, looking around, spied them lazing in the sun. He tiptoed down the steps and across the grass, but they heard him coming and began to thump their tails. And, after chomping down the treats, they rolled onto their backs for belly rubs. "You guys are silly, you know that?" he said. When he stood up, he felt his leg muscles protest. "Ouch! Guess I'm not as young as I used to be!" The dogs' tails beat the ground in happy agreement.

Linden no longer noticed how much he talked to himself. It was a habit he'd picked up on the trail, and now, living alone, he did it all the time. If he wasn't talking to himself he was talking to whichever animal happened to be nearby. They were all rescues, except for the chickens, who had arrived at the post office in a loudly peeping box. But all of the others had a story to tell, and in return for Linden's kindness, they listened to his quiet rambling with profound compassion. Linden liked to think they understood every word.

He walked toward the barn, thinking about the work he was starting the next day. It was an ancient, winding stone wall that declared the boundaries and divided the pastures of an old dairy farm in neighboring Dublin. The farmer, old Will Harris, had died the previous October and a gentleman from New York had bought the property as a weekend retreat from the city.

Linden lifted several rings of hose from the rack, dropped them to the ground, and lifted the pump handle. Water splashed onto the ground and splattered his jeans. He tipped the water trough, gave it a quick scrub, and filled it with fresh water. The cows trundled over, followed by the inquisitive little mule that waited patiently for the cows to finish. Linden held the hose out to him and he curiously stuck his long, gray tongue into the stream of water, but when it splashed into his cavernous nostrils, he turned away. "You're such an e.e. ore!" Linden teased affectionately, scratching his boney head.

Turning his attention back to the cows, Linden stroked Reba's belly and remembered the first time he'd heard about the plight of the Randall breed. He'd been walking through the cow barn at the Tunbridge Fair and had stopped to admire the unusual lineback coloring of the two cows that were munching contentedly in the last stall. A young woman, standing nearby, had handed him a pamphlet.

"They're pretty, aren't they?" she'd said with a warm smile. Linden had nodded, and accepted the pamphlet. "They're purebred, native to Sunderland. They were originally bred by a farmer named Everett Randall. The problem is, their numbers are dwindling." She had looked Linden over. "Are you a dairy farmer?"

"Me?!" Linden had laughed, but when he left the dairy barn that day, he'd had the pamphlet tucked in his pocket with Cindy's phone number on it, and he'd had something new to think about. A couple of months later, a rickety cattle trailer had pulled into the yard with Reba and Rosie inside, and Reba was already pregnant.

Cindy had climbed out; looked at the fresh hay in the barn; admired the pretty, sun-swept meadow lined with stone walls; and declared, "This little place is perfect." They'd chatted over coffee, and then she'd climbed back into her old pickup, given one last look at the cows grazing in the Indian summer sun, and pulled away with her empty trailer rattling behind her. "Just call if you have any questions," she'd shouted. "I'll come down when she's close!"

She's getting close now, Linden thought. *Another week or so at most.* He wondered where he'd tucked Cindy's number, and he decided he'd better find it and put it near the phone. The cows, finally satisfied, moseyed away and e.e. ore pushed his nose into the water while Linden splashed the stream from the hose into the cats' bowl.

He pushed down the pump handle, lifted the hose back into place, brushed off his hands, and stepped into the dusty heat of the barn. Maude emerged from her favorite sunny spot and began to brush against his legs, purring loudly. He knelt down to talk to her, and she put her front paws on his knee and talked back. Out of the corner of his eye, he saw a small flash of gray fur scurry between two hay bales and said, "Looks like someone's *not* doing their job." Maude ignored his comment and pushed her orange head into the palm of his hand, purring contentedly. She finally hopped down, and Linden, respectful of his aching muscles, stood up slowly. He looked around the barn and decided that it definitely needed some attention too. He located his wheelbarrow leaning against the back wall and wheeled it around the old red pickup that was parked in one of the bays. When he'd first moved in, Mr. Coleman had explained, with a slow sigh, that he hoped to restore the truck someday. Linden had nodded knowingly.

He set the wheelbarrow down outside the first stall and reached for a pitchfork that was hanging on the rack. A dusty transistor radio was sitting on a crossbeam next to the tools, and Linden clicked it on. He adjusted the antenna and turned the knob slightly to tune in the local rock station. The announcer was just finishing the weekend sports report, and Linden listened with mild interest.

"As for all you NASCAR fans, in case you weren't paying attention, Saturday night turned out to be the Dale and Dale show with Dale Jarrett pulling off the win at the Pepsi 400 and Dale Earnhardt following him around under caution, coming in second. After the win, Jarrett's car ran out of gas and his pit crew had to push him into Victory Lane!"

Linden smiled at the thought of the 88 car being *pushed* into victory lane. As he began to scoop manure, he wondered if Mr. Wyeth still followed the races. Linden knew he was a die-hard Earnhardt fan, although he also liked Jarrett. Linden would never forget the race he'd gone to with Callie and her dad. It was up in Loudon and their seats had been right on the front stretch. Linden could still hear the deafening rumble of the engines and feel the rush of adrenaline as the cars roared by.

It had always seemed to Linden that his relationship with Callie had started to unravel after that summer. They'd gone back to college, knowing they probably wouldn't see each other until Thanksgiving, and then her mom had been in the accident.

Linden had attended the funeral with his parents and, even though it had been a cold and rainy November day, the little church had been overflowing with friends and former patients, everyone realizing just how many people Ginny Wyeth's life had touched. Mr. Wyeth had been a pillar of strength—everyone had said so—but Callie had been inconsolable. Linden had hugged her and told her how sorry he was, and she'd nodded tearfully. And then he'd just stood there, feeling foolish, not knowing what else to say. Callie hadn't returned to school, and the college had sent her a note of sympathy telling her she'd be welcomed back whenever she felt ready. Linden had stopped by several times when he was home, but Callie had still seemed lost and sad. She'd tried to smile at his cheering words, but her eyes had always looked like they were ready to spill over with tears. He'd begun to wonder if she'd ever feel better. Finally, at her dad's gentle insistence, she'd reluctantly returned to school after the winter break.

Linden had not seen Callie again until February, and then it was only briefly. Thankfully, she'd seemed more herself and had even said she and some friends were making plans to go somewhere warm for spring break, adding, with a sad smile, that she really needed to get away. Linden hadn't seen her again until she came home for the Connors' Fourth of July party.

He finished cleaning the stalls and began straightening up the hay bales. Perspiration dripped down his cheeks, and hay dust coated his skin. He sneezed, pulled off his shirt, wiped his face with it, and decided that he didn't feel like doing much of anything. He stepped outside, soaked his head under the hose, shook his hair, and ran his hands through it to push it back. Cool beads of water trickled down his back. He sat down on the stone wall in the shade and looked out across the meadow. The tall, billowing clouds reminded him of the Eric Sloane painting his parents had hanging over their fireplace.

18

Callie drove slowly around the hospital parking lot again, but the only spot she could find was near the emergency room. She finally parked in it, but when she got out she realized, in dismay, that it was the same spot her father had slid into the night her mom had died. Everything had been coated in a sheet of ice that night, and he'd pulled in so quickly that the truck had just kept sliding, stopping only when it rested against the lamppost. Callie glanced down. Although it had been painted, there was still a visible dent. She stared at it and realized that her memory of that night would always be a blur of sadness and disbelief.

She'd come home from college the day before Thanksgiving, and she and her mom spent that evening making pies, laughing, and catching up. Even though her mom had to work on Thanksgiving, she and her dad would go to the hospital, as they always did when her mom had to work a holiday, and have dinner with her in the cafeteria. They'd have the pies to look forward to when she finally got home.

A light snow had started to fall that afternoon and, even though the weatherman had said it wasn't supposed to amount to much, by the time Callie and her dad had returned from the dinner, it was really coming down. As soon as they walked in the house her dad had picked up the phone, and Callie had stood in the kitchen, still wearing her jacket, waiting and listening.

"I'm sorry to call you at work, hon'," he'd said, "but I'm concerned about the roads. I think you might want to wait before you head home, or else I can come back in the truck." He paused, and

Callie could tell her mom wasn't easily convinced. Finally, it was her dad who relented. "Well, okay, but promise me you'll turn around if the roads are bad. Yes, love you too." He had hung up the phone and stood by the window, watching the snow fall.

On a normal day, her mom would have left work at three-thirty and been home by four. But that afternoon, four-thirty came and went, and by five it was getting dark. Callie and her dad had tried to watch football, but neither one knew who was playing, never mind who was winning. Her dad had turned on the outside lights and realized that the snow had changed to a wintry mix. He had reached for his coat and announced he was going to look for her, and Callie had stood up and said she wanted to go too. But her dad had said it would be better if she stayed by the phone.

He was still clearing the snow off his truck when the state trooper pulled up at the end of the driveway with his vehicle's emergency lights glowing in the misty darkness. Callie had watched from the kitchen door as he got out, put on his covered hat, and walked up the driveway toward her father. She had felt icy fingers of fear wrap around her heart as she watched her dad turn to talk to him; her dad had nodded and his shoulders had sagged, and then she'd stumbled out to stand beside him.

Her memory, after that, was a confused jumble

of images and voices: the solemn look on the officer's face, the pelting ice stinging her cheeks, shivering in the darkness. Her dad putting his arm around her, telling her to go get her coat . . . but not being able to move . . . just shaking uncontrollably . . . and not being able to breathe . . . just drowning in the sea of words. *Mrs. Wyeth was traveling on Mountain Road . . . a sharp corner . . . a slight incline . . . a boy from Maine heading in the opposite direction . . . lost control . . . both rushed by ambulance . . . the boy was pretty banged up . . . but Mrs. Wyeth was much worse . . . did they want him to drive them?*

No . . . No . . . Thank you. Her dad's face was pale and his hands were shaking. *They would take the truck. They were leaving now.*

Callie would never forget the eeriness of the emergency lights flashing across the dark, misty sky as they approached the accident scene. Her mom's car was already loaded on a flatbed, and the front of the boy's car was unrecognizable. She'd looked away, tears streaming down her cheeks, but when she'd spotted her mom's nursing cap lying in the snow, she'd screamed, *"Stop, Dad! Stop!"*

Henry slipped his hand into Callie's, and she looked down and suddenly remembered why they were there. She scooped him up, and he touched the tear on her cheek. It dribbled down his finger.

Callie wiped her face and smiled. "It's okay, Hen-Ben. Mommy's just thinking too much . . . *again*." She reached for the paper bag with the sandwich in it. "Let's go see Papa."

They walked down the corridor toward her dad's room and, as she passed the nurses' station, an unfamiliar face looked up. "May I help you?"

"We're just on our way to see my dad."

The nurse looked down at the list of patients. "I'm sorry, but which patient is your dad?"

Henry started to squirm in Callie's arms, and Callie, becoming impatient, shifted him to her other hip and answered, "Ben Wyeth."

Before the nurse could inquire further, another nurse bustled out of a nearby room and Callie was relieved to see a familiar face. Jess was one of her mom's former coworkers, and her friendly eyes lit up when she saw Callie, but then they quickly clouded over in a frown. "Oh, baby, we've been trying to reach you all morning."

Callie's relief turned to panic. "Why? What's wrong?"

"It's your daddy, honey. He's had another stroke." Jess wrapped her arms around both of them. "I'm so sorry," she whispered. When Jess pulled away, tears were streaming down Callie's cheeks. "Oh, baby, don't cry," she said, gently wiping away the tears. "You're going to upset this beautiful little boy." Jess smiled at Henry. "Your grampa's gonna be *okay*, honey. Don't you worry.

We're taking good care of him." Jess turned back to Callie. "He's been moved to intensive care."

Callie nodded, her body obviously straining under the unbearable weight of her world. "Thank you, Jess," she said.

"Girl, *what* is wrong with your phone? I was going to send Todd up there as soon as he got out of work."

"I've been trying to get it hooked up," Callie explained, "but they came when I wasn't home."

Jess nodded. "Well, you better straighten it out so we can reach you." She hesitated. "Listen, do you want to talk to one of the doctors? Because I can get one for you. . . ." Callie shook her head, and Jess put her arm around her again. "He's going to be okay, baby. Your daddy's a fighter. That's where *you* get it from." Callie smiled. "That's my girl." Jess smiled too. "Listen, you get a sitter and come back later and you can see him, okay?"

"Can't Henry see him?" Callie asked.

Jess shook her head. "No, baby, I thought you knew. Little people can't go into intensive care."

Callie swallowed hard and bit her lip. "No, I didn't know."

"Well, you'll have to get someone to watch him. I'm sorry, honey." Jess gave her another big hug. "Don't you worry," she whispered again, "your daddy's going to be just fine."

• • •

Henry refused to get back in the car. He squirmed and kicked and finally pulled his hand free, and then, before she could stop him, he ran headlong into the lamppost and fell back onto the hot pavement, holding his head and screaming at the top of his lungs.

"What is the matter with you?" Callie shouted. "Get up, for God's sake. What are you doing?" She wrenched his arm, pulled him to his feet, and shook him. "Look, Henry, cut it out! I can't take it anymore!" she shouted. "I just can't take it anymore!" Henry stomped his feet and began to slap his ears violently. "Stop!" she commanded, grabbing his wrists. "Stop doing that! Why can't you just be normal?" Callie heard the words spilling from her mouth but couldn't believe she was saying them. Henry fell into a heap next to the car, wrapped his arms around his knees, and rocked back and forth, whimpering.

"Is everything okay, Miss?" Callie looked up and saw an older gentleman crossing the parking lot toward them.

"Yes, we're fine," she answered, scooping Henry up. "We're just going for a walk." The man nodded and stood with his hands in the pockets of his white coat and watched them cross the street.

As they passed through the gates of the nearby cemetery, Callie wondered again why cemeteries in New England always seemed to be across from hospitals. It certainly wasn't a very promising scene for patients who looked out their windows or for the family members who kept watch at their bedsides. Callie pictured the early colonists carrying their deceased loved ones down the grassy hill and wondered if the cemetery's proximity to the hospital had everything to do with convenience. She put Henry down, and he wandered along between the sun-bleached headstones. To her surprise, he stayed near.

They came to a shady grove, and Callie stopped. The pines whispered softly around them, and Henry gazed at the simple white marker. He walked up to it and traced his finger lightly over the engraved letters:

VIRGINIA DEERING WYETH
JUNE 19, 1949–NOVEMBER 23, 1994
BELOVED WIFE ~ DEAR MOTHER
FOREVER FRIEND

Callie watched her son's innocent gesture and realized how much her mom would have loved him. She would have known what to do. She would have known how to reach him. She would have held him and hugged him and loved him with all her heart.

"Oh, Mom, I miss you so much," she whispered.

As she silently watched, Henry picked up a smooth, white stone and placed it on top of the headstone. As he stepped back, though, thunder rumbled ominously in the distance, and he reached for Callie's hand. She looked at the sky and felt the heavy stillness of the air. "Guess we should get going," she said reluctantly. She scooped him up onto her hip but lingered a moment more, and wished they'd brought flowers. "Next time," she whispered. A resounding crack echoed across the valley, and Henry whimpered. "It's okay, Hen-Ben," she said, hugging him. She ran her hand lightly along the headstone and then turned to hurry up the hill.

Just as they reached the car the skies opened up and, in the time it took to strap Henry in and run around to her side of the car, Callie was drenched. She dove into the front seat, quickly rolled up the windows, and decided to wait for the storm to pass. The rain thundered on the metal roof and streamed down the steamy glass. A rivulet formed on the inside of the windshield and trickled down, dripping on the dashboard. Over the years, her dad had tried several times to fix the leak, but when it rained hard enough, or when the wind blew just right, water always managed to find its way in.

Callie watched the fat droplets form and splash on the dusty dash and thought of Linden. She shook her head. *How can I even think of asking him? After everything that's happened, how can I ask the one person in the world that I hurt most to look after the child that resulted from that hurt?*

The irony is too much! She watched the lush trees swaying back and forth in a green blur and prayed, "Oh, God, help me. Please give me a sign."

The storm finally passed, and she looked in her rearview mirror. Henry was sound asleep. She started the car, drove slowly out of the parking lot, and headed east. When she turned onto Route 124, she began to notice that cars were pulling over. She looked in her rearview mirror and listened for a siren, but she didn't hear one. *Why are people pulling over?* She slowed down and watched as people got out of their cars. One person was even holding a camera. Finally, she looked up through the passenger window and spotted what everyone was looking at: A brilliant double rainbow was spanning the eastern sky.

19

The air was ominously still and heavy with moisture as Linden measured and cut the wood for the new treads, and it wasn't long before a distant rumble confirmed the approach of a summer storm. He made one final cut, fit the tread, glanced at the sky, and decided he'd better clean up his makeshift shop. He gathered his tools, brought them inside, and then hurried to the barn to usher the animals inside.

Twenty minutes later, an eerie darkness shrouded the yard. The dogs had been only too happy to be invited into the kitchen. They stretched out on the cool linoleum and wondered if there were any snacks in their future. Linden turned on the stove light, looked under the aluminum foil that covered Mrs. Connor's cookies, and shook his head in dismay. "Only two left. I don't know if there's enough." With their heads on their paws, the dogs watched Linden as he ate the first cookie, but when he started to lift the second one to his mouth, they picked up their heads and gave him mournful looks. Linden laughed, broke the cookie in half, and gave them each a piece. They thumped their tails thankfully. Linden poured milk into the glass from the dish drain, wandered into the small room next to the kitchen, and looked out at the rain. Even though it was coming down in sheets, he could already see a sliver of blue shimmering across the western horizon.

He finished his milk, turned from the window, and switched on the adjustable lamp that was attached to the old wooden drawing table. The table was solid oak and had been rescued from a Vermont roadside, and the threadbare swivel chair in front of it had come from a junkyard in Keene. Linden sat in the chair and ran his hand lightly over the watercolor that was taped to the table. He leaned away and then closer again, trying to decide if he liked it. Several weeks earlier, in frustration, he'd given up on the painting, but now he decided maybe it wasn't so bad. He stood up and looked at it from another angle. Maybe he'd work on it later.

The rain had stopped, and Linden let the dogs back out and carried a new six-pack down to the river. He slipped five of the bottles into the cold water, unbuttoned his shirt, dried his hands with it, draped it over the back of one of the chairs, and opened the remaining bottle. Then he kicked off his L.L.Bean camp mocs and made his way gingerly out across the shallow current. He stood, sipping his beer and surveying his handiwork. The cairn was almost as tall as he was, but he still wanted it to be taller. He began to wonder if spending so much time alone was making him crazy, and then he remembered an article he'd read one time that said if you thought you were crazy, you probably weren't. He put his bottle down; looked into the depths of the clear, swirling water; and realized that he'd almost exhausted his supply of large stones. He would have to start carrying them from upstream. He had just started to slosh in that direction when he heard a car pull into the yard.

He looked up and saw Callie's old Nova parked next to his truck and his heart pounded as he watched Kat and Springer bounding over to greet her. She petted them and looked around.

"Hey," he called with a wave.

She looked over and smiled. "Hey!"

"You remembered."

"Well, I thought I remembered, but I made a wrong turn back there"—she motioned in the direction of the road—"and I ended up at a wooden gate. But I finally figured it out." As she walked toward him, she couldn't help but notice that he was no longer the slender boy she'd known in high school. His chest and shoulders were broader, and his muscles were more defined. Linden reached for his shirt, and she quickly looked away, suddenly embarrassed.

"Wow! *That* is a very impressive pile of rocks," she said, looking over his shoulder.

Linden pulled the shirt on and thought, *If you only knew what inspired it!*

"I shouldn't have come," she stammered.

"No," Linden said, fumbling with a button. "I'm glad you did."

She searched his eyes. "I *really* shouldn't have come," she blurted, "but I don't have anywhere else to turn. I know you offered to help, Linden, but you probably didn't expect me to take you up on it so soon." She paused to take a breath. "Please say no if you can't . . . or you're busy . . . or you *just* don't want to. I will completely understand."

Linden gave up on the buttons and stepped closer. "Callie, what's the matter? What happened?" Callie started to explain, and Linden caught on immediately. "No problem, Cal. I'm happy to watch Henry."

She nodded and bit her lip. "It's not that simple, Linden," she continued. "Henry's not like other kids. He's not easy to look after. He takes off, and he has terrible tantrums and . . ." She paused, trying to find the right words. "He doesn't talk."

"Oh," Linden said. "Well, I'm sure we can manage. I do enough talking for two people anyway."

Callie looked puzzled. *"You?"*

Linden smiled and shrugged. "Did you want to leave him here now?"

"Is now okay?"

"Now is fine."

They walked over to Callie's car. "This is crazy. I can't believe I'm doing this to you. I don't even know how he will react to new surroundings, especially without me here. He's an escape artist, and he disappears in the blink of an eye. You have to watch him every second. Are you absolutely sure you want to do this?"

"Yes, I'm sure. We'll be fine." Linden insisted. He searched her eyes. "Your dad needs you too."

Callie leaned into the car and unstrapped Henry's car seat and woke him. As she lifted him out, he started to kick and scream, but when he saw Linden he immediately stopped.

"See," Linden said with a smile. "I have the magic touch."

"Yes, I know. . . ." She bit her lip again. "Well, we'll see if you still feel that way when I get back." She looked at Henry. "You're going to stay with Linden for a little while. I'll be back as soon as I can. Be good!" She turned to Linden. "Thank you so much."

20

As Callie pulled away, her mind raced with all the things that could go wrong and all the things she'd forgotten to mention about Henry. She looked at her watch and realized it was almost suppertime. *He's probably hungry . . . that alone could send him into a tailspin. And he probably needs to use the bathroom . . . what if he wets his pants? And then there's that river . . . why didn't I mention that he's never been in water deeper than a bathtub?* Callie began to wonder if she should go back. *What if something happens? Oh, God, please don't let anything happen! Please take care of them. . . .*

Callie tried not to worry as she hurried down the hall toward the nurses' station. She glanced at her watch and realized the evening shift must have taken over, because she didn't recognize a soul. A nurse looked up from her clipboard, and Callie asked her if it would be okay to visit Ben Wyeth. The nurse scanned the list of patients as Callie tried to read the list upside down. Just then, a doctor pushed through the swinging double doors at the end of the hall, and the nurse stood up. He was looking down at a chart, but Callie immediately recognized him as the older gentleman in the white coat who had approached her in the parking lot. She turned away quickly, hoping he wouldn't recognize her, but the nurse said, "Dr. Franklin, this young lady would like to visit Mr. Wyeth." She turned back to Callie. "Are you his daughter?" Callie nodded, and the doctor held out his hand and smiled.

"I'm Dr. Franklin."

"I'm Callie Wyeth," she replied, taking his hand.

The doctor looked puzzled. "Were you in the parking lot this afternoon with your little boy?"

Callie felt her cheeks flush. "Yes, I can explain . . ."

"There's no need," he said kindly. "Let's go sit down. Your dad is resting, and I could use a cup of coffee. Would you like one?"

"Oh . . . okay. . . ." Callie stammered.

The doctor led Callie to a quiet corner off the hall that was furnished with chairs and a sofa. "How do you take your coffee?" he asked. Moments later, he returned with two steaming cups of black coffee.

"Thank you," Callie said, cradling the cup in her hands.

Dr. Franklin nodded, his blue eyes sparkling behind his glasses. He was tall and lanky, and his kind face was framed with snowy-white sideburns that crept up into a shock of reddish-blond hair. He explained that he was the heart specialist and he'd been in the ER when they'd brought Ben in. "I had a chance to spend some time with your dad yesterday, and I've already heard several old navy stories." He smiled wistfully. "He reminds me of my dad, who was also a gifted storyteller *and* retired navy."

Callie smiled. She knew how much her father loved to tell stories and jokes. She'd heard some of them more times than she could count.

Dr. Franklin leaned forward and put his elbows on his knees. "Your dad is far from out of the woods, Callie," he said gently. "He is stable, and we are treating him with medication, but when he's stronger he'll need surgery." Callie nodded, and the doctor explained how stents would help open up her father's blocked arteries.

Finally, he leaned back and took a sip of his coffee. He looked intently in Callie's eyes, paused for a moment, and then said gently, "I have a son with autism."

Callie stared. "You do?"

He nodded. "Several years ago, my wife and I moved up here from New Haven because we thought life in the country would be easier for him, and it has been." He paused. "What's your son's name?"

"Henry," Callie replied with a half smile.

The doctor smiled too. "That's a good name." He paused. "So, how're you doing? You seemed to be having a tough moment in the parking lot." Callie nodded. "It's not easy. When he's upset, I don't know if he's feeling overwhelmed or if he's just being difficult, *and* I really wish I knew if he will always be this way."

Dr. Franklin nodded thoughtfully. "Every child is different, but you'll learn how to tell what's triggering his behavior—if he's overtired or overstimulated—and you'll learn how to help him by controlling his environment. It's impossible to know if he'll always be the way he is now, but there are definitely things you can do to make it easier for both of you. Children with autism like order and they like to know what's coming next, so you should try to stick to a routine that he can count on, play games that involve taking turns, be firm and consistent with discipline, but most importantly, be patient. Eventually, he will learn what is expected of him." He stood up, and Callie stood too. "Our son was diagnosed eighteen years ago and, at the time, even less was known about autism. My wife and I learned by trial and error." He paused and smiled. "Sometimes, Callie, you'll feel like you're the only one in the world who's struggling with this but, believe me, you're not."

"Thank you, Dr. Franklin." Callie said, reaching out to shake his hand. "Thank you for taking the time."

The doctor smiled and took her hand, and then put his arm around her shoulder. "Now, go see your dad."

Just then, another doctor came down the hall. "Henry!" he exclaimed. "I've been looking all over for you. Are you ready to go to dinner?" Dr. Franklin looked at Callie and smiled again. "Call me if you have any questions . . . day or night. And, when your dad is stronger, we'll talk more about surgery."

21

Kat and Springer were delighted by the arrival of their new guest. When Linden put Henry down, they discovered he was the perfect height, and they did their very best to make him feel welcome. Henry crinkled his brow as they wiggled around him, sniffing every inch of his small frame, licking his cheeks, and snorting in his ears. Finally, Henry reached out timidly and placed his hands on their heads. The dogs responded by wiggling even more, and Linden couldn't help but laugh.

Henry trundled toward the porch with his two new escorts and sat on the top step. The dogs followed and lay down on either side of him, still sniffing. Henry seemed content to run his hands over their soft fur, and Linden thought, after all of Callie's cautionary words, looking after Henry seemed pretty easy. He leaned back in one of the wicker chairs and continued to watch them.

Finally, he asked, "Henry, are you hungry?"

At the question, Henry stood, and Linden took that to mean yes. They went inside and Linden showed him where the bathroom was, just in case. To his surprise, Henry knew what to do, and while he did it, Linden fed the dogs. When Henry didn't come right out, though, Linden went to check on him. He found him standing in front of the counter, lining up his shaving cream, toothbrush holder, soap dispenser, toothpaste, and anything that was within reach. "Hey," he said, and Henry looked up. "I thought you were hungry." Henry put down the stack of Dixie cups he was holding and followed Linden into the kitchen. Linden had cut up an apple and put it in a bowl with a dollop of peanut butter, and after Henry scooted onto a chair, Linden showed him how to dip the apple into the peanut butter. "This is one of my favorite snacks," he said with his mouth full. "Fluff is good too." Henry caught on right away, immediately dipping a slice of apple into the peanut butter and nibbling on it. Linden poured a small glass of milk, and Henry drank that down too. "Guess you are hungry," he said. While Henry ate the apple, the dogs lay at his feet, watching him. "You'll have to excuse Kat and Springer," Linden explained. "They're incorrigible beggars *and* they love apples." Henry dipped a slice of apple into the peanut butter and held it out to Kat. She took it gently, and then Springer pushed his nose into Henry's lap too. Linden watched as Henry dipped a second slice for Springer. It was obvious to Linden that Henry understood every word he said.

When he was finished eating, Linden put the cup and bowl in the sink and asked, "Want to help feed the other animals?" Henry crinkled his brow as he slid off the chair but stood ready to follow. Linden pushed open the door, and the dogs pulled themselves up from the slippery floor and trotted out. Henry followed and, as they crossed the yard, he slipped his small hand into Linden's. Linden looked down in surprise and smiled.

As they neared the barn, Henry's eyes grew wide when he saw Reba's big head leaning over the fence, reaching for several tall sprigs of alfalfa that were waving in the breeze. Her long tongue finally curled around the sweet grass, and she pulled it back and munched contentedly. When a second big head leaned over the fence, though, Henry stopped in his tracks and gripped Linden's hand more tightly. Linden reassured him, "It's okay, Henry. They're friendly." As he said this, a big gray cat sauntered out of the barn and the orange tiger cat hopped up on the stone wall and sat down to wash her paws. "Everybody," Linden announced, "this is Henry." He looked down at Henry and said, "Henry, this is everybody." He pointed to each animal and said its name. "That's Reba, and that's Rosie; the little mule over there is e.e. ore; and that's Maude, and this is Harold," he said as the gray cat brushed against his legs. "And, up in the rafters of the barn is Atticus. Let's go see if he's in there." Henry followed Linden into the barn, and Linden pointed up to the uppermost beam. The old brown owl blinked down at them, and Henry nodded ever so slightly. Linden noticed him nod and wondered if he communicated in ways other than talking.

"Okay, the cats get a little kibble at suppertime," he said, opening a small plastic bin, "even though"—he looked around and announced loudly—"they're supposed to be feasting on mice." He held out a cup to Henry. "Want to put this in their dishes?" Henry took the cup and carefully poured half into each dish and then handed the cup back to Linden. "Good job," Linden said, nodding. They walked back outside, and Linden lifted the hose off its rack. He gave one end of the hose to Henry and pointed to the trough. When Henry had the hose over it, he turned it on, and Henry filled it. Next, Linden lifted the top off of an old metal can. "The cows and e.e. don't get grain every night," Linden explained, "but tonight's a special occasion." He handed Henry a big scoop and pointed to three grain pails. Henry poured a little into each one and then stumblingly backed away as they all trundled toward him. Linden smiled and added, "No storms are headed our way, so they can stay out tonight. But the chickens like to be inside, safe and cozy." He motioned to the henhouse, and Henry walked over and peered into the shadows at all the sleepy, quietly clucking ladies. Linden gently closed and latched the door. "Thanks, Henry. *You* are a big help."

22

Callie slipped quietly into her dad's room. A nurse was taking his blood pressure, but when she heard Callie come in, she looked up and smiled. Callie was surprised to see the curtains open and the evening sun filling the room with its warm, friendly light.

"Hey, Dad," she said softly.

Ben opened his eyes. "Hey there, kiddo."

"How're you feelin'?"

"A little tired," he replied honestly.

The nurse finished jotting down his numbers and said she'd be right back with his dinner. Ben nodded and turned to Callie. "I'm sorry to put you through all this."

"Don't be sorry, Dad, you're not putting me through anything."

"Yes, I am," he said, reaching for her hand. "And you already have enough going on."

"It's okay, really. We're managing."

Ben tried to look around the room. "Hey, where's my pal?"

"Little kids can't come into intensive care."

"Oh." He paused. "That's a dumb rule. Where is he then?"

Now it was Callie's turn to pause. Finally, she said softly, "He's with Linden."

Ben's brow furrowed, and Callie wondered if *that* was where Henry had inherited that trait.

"Linden?"

Callie nodded and recounted their unexpected encounter in the hardware store, and then again outside the hardware store.

Ben nodded solemnly. "He's a good guy, Cal."

"I know, Dad, but I don't know how he can ever forgive what I did."

"You might be surprised."

Callie was quiet, lost in her own thoughts and still worried about leaving Henry. They talked for a bit, but when the nurse came back with his dinner she said, "I think I'm going to go. Can you manage?" He nodded, and she turned on the television for him. "I'm sorry, Dad. I'm just worried about him."

"Of course. Go. And don't feel like you have to come every day. I know you have your hands full."

Callie nodded and then hesitated. "Dad, I hate to ask you this, but would it be possible to borrow some money?"

Concern swept across Ben's face and, without hesitation, he said, "Of course. In the back of my closet. Take whatever you need—it's all yours anyway."

Callie frowned. "Not yet, it isn't."

Ben smiled. "I'm keeping you guys in my prayers."

Callie hugged him. "I'm praying for you too," she whispered.

Callie walked down the hall and silently said a prayer for her dad to get better. As she murmured amen, she wondered how many people actually remembered to say a prayer after saying they would. She shook her head. *If they're anything like me, they forget!* She walked to her car, still thinking about it. *And, if they're anything like me, they start off praying but end up thinking about what they're going to have for breakfast and then not even get to amen before they're getting out a cereal bowl.* Her dad had often said, "Prayer takes focus," and Callie knew it was true. As she pulled out of the parking lot, she wondered if what her dad had said about Linden forgiving her might also be true.

She thought back to the first Thanksgiving after her mom had died, when the only thing in the world she'd wanted was her dad's forgiveness. She'd stayed in Vermont that fall, even though she knew her dad was lonely. She ached to see him too, but she just couldn't face him. She was afraid of his reaction, of his anger; but more than anything, she was afraid of seeing the sadness in his eyes. The first time she'd seen disappointment in her dad's eyes, she was in second grade and had come home from school with a new pencil case. He'd asked her where she'd gotten it, and she'd stumbled over her answer, not knowing her teacher had called; not knowing he already knew the truth; not knowing that "I found it" was not the answer he was hoping for. But after she'd murmured those exact words, she'd watched in dismay as sadness and disappointment had filled his eyes, and she'd vowed she'd never see that look again.

When she pulled into the driveway on that Thanksgiving, though, she was seven months pregnant and she still hadn't told him. Tears had filled her eyes when she saw him standing in the doorway waiting for her.

Oh, God, please let him forgive me.

Biting her lip, she'd eased from the car and stood, pulling her coat around her round form. And her father, who had started walking across the driveway to greet her, had stopped and slowly shook his head in disbelief, trying to understand, trying to grasp what she hadn't shared with him.

At that sad moment, Callie had suddenly realized that *not* telling him had been a greater betrayal. She'd bowed her head in grief and shame as tears had spilled down her cheeks.

The rest of that day and the next had been quiet and tense. It was the first anniversary of her mom's accident and, just when her dad needed her most, he could hardly bring himself to look at her. Callie was devastated. "Please forgive me, Dad," she'd said quietly. Without looking up, he'd nodded. Despite his nod and the hug he gave her when she left, Callie had felt lost and alone when she returned to the old Vermont Victorian in which she rented an upstairs apartment.

One week later, though, she'd heard a sound outside her window and looked out to see him pulling up in front of the house. Tied down in the back of his pickup were her old baby crib, a new bassinet, a changing table, and a case of newborn-size diapers. She'd knocked on the window, and he'd looked up and smiled. Moments later, he'd come up the stairs lugging a box full of toys and clothes, and on top of the box was her old baby quilt, freshly laundered. He'd put the box down, given her a quick hug, taken a minute to catch his breath, and headed back down the stairs.

In spite of Callie's protests, he'd single-handedly carried all the furnishings up the stairs and insisted that Callie stay put and not lift a thing. While he set up the crib and changing table in her bedroom, she unpacked some of the clothes and toys. In the bottom of one of the boxes she found her old favorite bear and, with a smile, she'd gently propped him up in the corner of the crib.

Later on, as the melancholy sun peeked between the campus buildings, they'd ordered a pizza and sat together in her tiny kitchen to eat. Before he left, he'd wrapped her in a bear hug and told he'd always love her. No matter what.

And, one month later, on a snowy January night, he traveled through the darkness to be there when his new grandson was born. Callie had smiled as she watched him lift the tiny bundle into his arms and whisper, "Henry Benjamin Wyeth! *You* are beautiful! Oh, how I wish your grandmother were here to meet you!"

23

Linden and Henry were sitting on the stone wall, each with a single long piece of grass between his teeth, watching the cows graze when Callie pulled up. She breathed a sigh of relief to see Henry still there *and* seemingly content! She got out of the car, and Kat and Springer, who had been lazing in the late-day sun, pulled themselves up and trotted over to greet her. She knelt down, and they wiggled around her happily. Callie smiled. "This is, by far, the warmest welcome I've ever had!"

Linden nodded. "Well, they *are* the self-appointed welcoming committee."

"They're beautiful. What are their names?"

Linden smiled. "That big moose is Springer, and the smaller one is Kat."

"Cat?" Callie looked puzzled.

Linden nodded. "With a K, short for Katahdin."

"Like the mountain?"

"Yup, Springer is a mountain too." He paused. "They mark the beginning and end of the Appalachian Trail."

She looked over at Henry and smiled. "So? How'd it go?"

"Piece of cake," Linden said with a grin.

"No!" Callie said in surprised disbelief.

Linden nodded. "Yup, he was no problem, and he seemed to enjoy helping me with the animals." He paused. "By the way, I know you said he doesn't talk, but does he nod when he understands something?"

Callie looked puzzled and shook her head slowly. "Not that I've noticed," she answered skeptically. "Of course, I'm usually pretty good at upsetting him, so all I get are tantrums and revolutions."

Linden shrugged. "Well, I'm pretty sure he nodded, and he definitely understands everything I say." He paused thoughtfully. "How's your dad?"

Callie sat down next to Henry. "He seemed good, tired though. He was having supper when I left." She looked at Henry. "Speaking of which, I didn't even warn you that Henry might be hungry or that he might need the bathroom."

"We had a snack *and* I showed him where the bathroom is," Linden said with a smile. "I'm smarter than I look," he teased. "*And* I was a little guy once too."

Callie tried to picture Linden as "a little guy," and smiled. Unfortunately, their history didn't go back that far.

Linden interrupted her thoughts. "How 'bout you? Have you had supper?"

Callie looked over and shook her head. "Not yet, but I don't want to take up any more of your time. Besides, don't you need to get back to your project?" she asked, nodding toward the river.

"It can wait," Linden replied, suddenly remembering the beer he'd left out on a rock.

"Well, I'd love to treat *you* to dinner, Linden," she said with a sigh. "It's the least I can do, but Henry doesn't do very well in restaurants."

Linden looked over at the little boy sitting on the wall. He hadn't moved since Callie arrived. He just sat quietly, watching the cows. Linden followed his gaze and suddenly realized how much he wanted Callie to stay.

"We could order a pizza," he suggested.

Callie looked over. "Are you sure?"

He nodded.

"Okay, but I'm paying," she said, and then

remembered she didn't have any money. "I mean, I'm paying you back."

Linden smiled. "We'll see."

While they waited for the pizza to arrive, Linden introduced Callie to all of the animals and explained how each one had come to live with him. Callie listened attentively and realized that Linden was still the same tenderhearted boy she'd known in high school, ever willing to help and always the first to offer. As they walked back toward the cabin, the one resident who hadn't been introduced swooped out of the barn and settled in the tall Norway spruce across the meadow, his stately form silhouetted against the dusky sky. Henry pointed, and Linden tousled his hair. "Yup, that's Atticus."

"Atticus?" Callie asked, thinking back to their tenth-grade English class, and raising her eyebrows.

Linden grinned. "Atticus was already a resident *with* a name when I moved in," he said, "and I'm sure you can guess who named him."

Callie laughed. "I think that was one of Mr. Coleman's favorite books."

Linden nodded. "That and *Our Town*."

A noisy, green Plymouth Horizon rumbled into the driveway. "Did you order a pizza?" the driver called through his window. Linden nodded and pulled his wallet from his pocket as he walked toward the car. "This place is really tucked away," the driver commented, hoping for a big tip. Linden gave him an extra five. "Thanks, man!" the driver said with a grin as he pulled away.

"So, what do you think?" Linden asked, turning to Callie. "Shall we eat on the porch?"

"Sounds good," she replied.

Linden handed the box to her and quickly rearranged the wicker chairs and side table. "How 'bout a beer?"

Callie smiled. "Sure. I can't remember the last time I had a beer."

"Milk for Henry?"

"If you have enough. Do you need help?"

"Nope," he said, disappearing inside. Moments later, he reappeared with two bottles tucked under his arm, a small glass of milk, paper plates, napkins, and a crate for Henry to sit on. Callie opened the pizza box and slid slices onto the plates, and Linden put one on the table for Henry. Springer plopped down next to Henry and, before long, he had a sloppy string of drool hanging from his jowls. Linden shook his head in dismay. "Springer, try to pull yourself together." The big yellow Lab looked up at the mention of his name, thumped his tail hopefully, and turned his attention back to Henry. Callie watched Henry take another bite and realized that he hadn't fussed the whole time they were there.

An awkward silence fell over the porch, and Callie listened to the incessant buzz of insects in the trees. She was about to ask Linden how his parents were when another sound drifted across the meadow. Henry looked out into the inky darkness, and Linden smiled. "That's Atticus," he said softly. "Do you know what he's saying?" Henry furrowed his brow, and Linden continued, "He's saying, *'Who cooks for you? Who cooks for you aaaall?'*" Callie watched Henry nod and caught her breath as Linden went on, "If you keep listening, maybe his lady friend will answer." Moments later, they heard another owl calling from far away, *Who cooks for you? Who cooks for you?* Henry pointed, and Callie remarked in surprise, "It does sound like that's what they're saying!"

Linden nodded. "I heard a lot of owls when I hiked the AT." He leaned back and took a sip of his beer. "We also had a close encounter with a moose when we crossed into Maine." He looked at the dogs. "Didn't we, guys?" He stroked Kat's head. "He was big." Then he looked at Callie. "My two protectors were so brave, they just peeked at him through my legs!" He grinned affectionately at the dogs. "You guys had my back, right?" The dogs thumped their tails again in happy agreement. Henry reached out and gave them each a piece of pizza crust and Linden teased him, "You know, Henry, if you keep feeding them, they might follow you home." Henry nodded and gave them each another piece. Linden just laughed, but Callie shook her head.

"Don't give him any ideas!"

They were quiet for a while, and Henry pushed his plate away, climbed down, and nestled between the two dogs, contentedly stroking their soft fur.

Callie sighed. "I guess we should get going." She paused thoughtfully. "Linden, this was great. Thank you."

24

It was well past Henry's bedtime when Callie pulled into the driveway. She slipped his seat belt over his head and carried him inside. He was not happy about it, though, and he stomped his feet when she stood him in front of the toilet. "Go," she said, and he went—all over the back of the seat. She quickly realized he was still half asleep and not even aiming, so she reached around to help. When he was done, she propped him on the counter, washed his hands and face, carried him to the bedroom, slipped on his pajamas, and gently laid him down, covering only his legs with the sheet.

Callie had never liked the design of windows in ranch-style homes: Although they could be left open on rainy days, they always seemed to block the breeze and, since they were usually installed four feet above the floor, any air current that did slip in was well above the height of a bed. She pushed the bracket of Henry's window out all the way and hoped that the fans were still in the basement. Before going to look, though, she knelt beside his bed and whispered his prayer.

"Now I lay me down to sleep. I pray the Lord my soul to keep.
Thy love go with me through the night and wake me up in the morning light.
God bless me and Mom, help Papa get better . . . and bless Linden.
Amen."

She tucked Travelin' Bear near him and gently kissed his warm forehead. Then she went to the basement to look for the fans and the tools she would need to install the eyehooks. She came back up lugging two old floor fans and set one up in Henry's room, oscillating on low, and the second one in the living room. With the fan drawing cool air in from outside, she picked up the remote, aimed it at the TV, and pushed the power button. Nothing happened, so she walked over and turned it on manually. The eleven o'clock news was just ending and the weatherman was giving a quick recap: "It's going to be hot and humid all week with a line of severe thunderstorms coming through on Friday. Summer is in full swing now, and we'll feel it this week, except in the mountains, where it'll be a good ten degrees cooler." The anchorman smiled and tapped his pen. "Sounds like it will be a good week to head up to the Presidentials for a hike!" The weatherman nodded in agreement.

Callie sighed. "Great! Another hot week," she mumbled as she retreated to the kitchen to look for the eyehooks, but they were nowhere to be found. She wondered if she'd left them in the car. She located a flashlight in a drawer and pushed the switch, but it only flickered weakly and went out. She sighed in frustration and riffled through the junk drawer, looking for batteries. She found a pen and paper instead and, after she got the pen to work, she used it to scrawl the word *batteries* in bold letters across the top of the paper. Then she went outside and felt around in the car until she found the paper bag with the eyehooks in it under the passenger seat.

As she walked back to the house, she thought she heard an owl and paused to listen. It called several times, but there was never a reply. Finally, she went inside, dumped the eyehooks on the counter, and pushed a chair over to the door. She wanted the hooks to be within her reach but well out of Henry's. As she stood on the chair in the brightly lit house, listening to the TV, and working on her project, she realized her heart felt lighter than it had in months. It felt good to be home.

The next morning, she was up with the sun and, even though she'd stayed up late, she felt better rested than she had in a long time. She peeked in on Henry. He was curled up with Travelin' Bear tucked between his chest and his knees, and he was completely uncovered. She switched off his fan and slipped quietly to the kitchen to make coffee. While it perked cheerfully, she went back down the hall to take a quick shower, feeling much more at ease now that the doors were hooked.

She closed the bathroom door and slipped off the faded J.Crew pink boxers and white T-shirt that she always wore to bed in the summer. And while she waited for the water to warm up, she stood on her parents' old metal scale. The needle bounced up, danced a little, and settled on 104. Six pounds lighter than she'd weighed in high school. *That's what stress will do,* she thought. Stepping off the scale, she reached around the shower curtain to check the water temp and caught a glimpse of herself in the mirror. She couldn't remember when she'd last seen her reflection in a full-length mirror. She reached up self-consciously and tucked several strands of long blond hair behind her ear, and sighed. *As out of control as ever!* She ran her fingertip lightly along the outline of the tan bib she always had in the summer, and then she looked down. Slowly, she ran her hand over her flat stomach and studied her thighs. Then she turned. *Not much change there, but how long will it last without exercise? Maybe I should get one of those baby joggers.*

She opened the bathroom door and listened. The

house was quiet, so she dropped her towel within reach of the tub, left the door open a crack, and climbed in. The warm water felt refreshing, and she finally relaxed. While she washed, she pictured Linden and wondered what he was doing at that moment.

Twenty minutes later she was in the kitchen, sipping coffee and rinsing blueberries. She'd bought two pints the day before with the hope of making muffins. She'd just started grating lemon zest when Henry wandered into the kitchen, rubbing his eyes. "Good morning, buddy," she said. "Did you remember to go to the bathroom?" Henry made a face and stomped his foot, and she knew he hadn't. "Could you please go?" she asked gently, but he ignored her, and wandered into the living room. Callie rinsed her hands and followed him. "Let's go," she said firmly. He pretended he didn't hear her, so she picked him up, but he squirmed and kicked violently. "We can do this the easy way or we can do it the hard way," she said, struggling with him. As she carried him down the hall, though, he swung around and knocked one of the pictures off the wall. Callie looked down at the spider web of broken glass over a portrait of her parents and clenched her jaw. She closed her eyes and, through gritted teeth, whispered, "Please help me *not* lose it."

She continued down the hall, set Henry in front of the toilet, and roughly pulled his pajama shorts down. "Go," she said sternly, but he just stood there with his arms crossed. She continued in the same firm tone. "Henry, if you *don't* go, I am going to take away your LEGOs." With that, a steady stream hit the water. After she made sure he washed his hands, she went back down the hall and picked up the portrait.

Henry looked at the picture and pointed. "Don't touch," she said, pushing his hand away. "The glass is sharp. It can cut." He reached out to point again. "Henry, did you hear me?" she said sharply. His brow furrowed, and he clenched his fists. Callie looked at his face, trying to understand. Then she looked at the picture and said, "That's Papa when he was younger, and this is Grandma." She paused, not knowing what else to say. *How do I explain who this lovely lady is? And how do I explain why she isn't a part of our lives?* "She was *my* mom," she said finally, her heart aching with renewed grief. She put the picture on the kitchen counter and threw away the broken glass, the pieces crashing together as they fell into the pail.

She turned back to the muffins, poured milk into the bowl of sifted ingredients, and asked him if he wanted to stir. He pushed a chair over and she handed him the spoon, and he immediately began to scrape it around the bowl, causing big puffs of flour and sugar to fly out. "Try to keep it *in* the bowl," she said, but he continued to stir with such vigor that the milk and eggs began splashing out

130

too. She grabbed his hand. "You are really testing me today!" she said angrily. In one sweeping motion he wrenched his hand away and threw the spoon across the kitchen. It sailed through the air, hit the window, cracking it, and clattered to the floor, leaving a trail of gooey batter in its wake. Callie grabbed both of his wrists and pulled him off the chair, and he immediately began to scream. "I'm really going to lose it, Henry!" she warned. "Cut it out!" She tried to pick him up, but he sprawled on the floor and continued to carry on. Callie turned away from him and stared out the window. "I thought *You* didn't give us any more than we can handle," she said, her voice choked with emotion.

With Henry still rocking back and forth on the floor, Callie thought about Linden's words, "He understands everything I say." *How can that be?* she wondered. *Did Linden communicate differently? How in the world did he get him to cooperate so easily?* She shook her head. She just didn't know how to communicate differently. She didn't know how to help him, and she definitely didn't know how much more *she* could take. "Please, show me what to do," she prayed.

Just then, there was a knock at the door, and Henry stopped crying and looked up. Standing outside the door was the telephone repairman. Callie unhooked the door and said, "I am so glad you're here."

25

When Linden pulled up in front of the old farmhouse the next morning, the sun was just peeking over the hill but a gently disheveled gentleman with white hair was already outside pulling weeds. He had the scholarly appearance of an Ivy League alum, but when Linden greeted him as *Mr.* Thompson, he held up his hand. "Please, Linden, call me Fairbanks." He wiped his hands on his wrinkled khaki pants, took off his round tortoiseshell glasses, rubbed them on the tattered T-shirt that hung carelessly below his threadbare white oxford, and reached out to shake hands, his blue eyes twinkling in the sunlight. Completing his outfit were gray argyle socks and worn buck shoes. *So this is how a writer lives,* Linden thought. They walked over and leaned against the split rail fence in the hazy sunshine to talk about the project.

"I don't want it to be perfect," Fairbanks said, absentmindedly taking off his glasses again and holding them up to the light. "No string lines or anything like that. I'd just like it to be restored to its original purpose: maintaining pastures and keeping in animals." Linden nodded, and Fairbanks suggested they walk a bit of the property so he could show Linden what he meant. "The frozen ground swell has damaged the wall, pushing the stones off and spilling the upper boulders into the sun," he said, pointing to a clutch of stones that had fallen on the grass.

Linden smiled. "Frost."

Fairbanks studied Linden and chuckled at his new friend's pun. "Yes, Frost *and* frost!"

Fairbanks Thompson was a nature editorialist, and his contributions to the *New York Times* were legendary among his peers, and well-loved by his readers. He'd also written several best-selling books, but he'd just begun considering retirement when his publisher suggested he write a memoir. The old man had been mulling the idea over while visiting friends in New England when he stumbled upon, and fell in love with, the old Dublin farmhouse. It was the perfect setting, he decided, to write a memoir.

When Linden and Fairbanks returned to the house, they shook hands again and Fairbanks said he'd be inside, trying to write, if Linden needed anything. As Linden climbed back into his truck, he called after him. "Young man, what do you know of Harlow's Pub?"

Linden smiled. "It's good."

The old gentleman nodded, running his hand through his untamed mane. "I have friends coming," he explained, his voice trailing off.

Linden waved as he pulled away. He drove up through the pastures and parked in the shade. When he climbed out, he looked back down at the farmhouse, feeling a bit envious of the writer's lifestyle. At one time, he'd dreamed of being an artist. In high school he had been the kid that drew all the posters for the school plays; in fact, he still had several of them tucked away in an old portfolio. His favorite was the one he'd designed for *Our Town*. It was a montage with a small New England town in the background, and on the lower left, the narrator was speaking and motioning with his hands; on the right side, Emily and George were walking together, and George was tossing a ball into the air. Everyone at the high school had raved about the poster and his ability to capture his classmates' likenesses. Several people had even asked him to sign their copies. After that, he'd been voted class artist, but when he mentioned going to art school instead of a liberal arts college, his mother wouldn't hear of it. He could still hear the derision in her voice. "*What* in the world would you do with an art degree?" she'd asked. In the end, much to her dismay, he'd ended up with no degree at all.

The day was hazy and hot, and Linden pulled his T-shirt over his head and dropped it onto the sunny grass. As he surveyed the wall, he noticed that every stone had a unique map of moss and lichen and, from the pattern, he could almost guess its previous position on the wall. He was glad Fairbanks didn't want him to use string. A true New England wall wasn't perfect. It wandered along where it was needed, its path determined by the landscape. If it encountered a tree, it went around it, and then it continued to follow the lay of the land.

Linden worked steadily, and by late morning his stomach was rumbling. He usually packed a couple of peanut butter and jelly sandwiches, but that morning he'd realized, too late, that he was out of bread, so he'd made a quick stop at the deli and treated himself to a ham and Swiss grinder with lettuce, tomato, mustard, and mayo. It was a welcome change and he devoured it quickly, washing it down with a quart of orange Gatorade. His voracious appetite had not diminished at all since high school, and sometimes he worried that, if his metabolism ever slowed down, he'd balloon into a much larger version of himself. He sighed, popped the second of three Oreos in his mouth, and decided he didn't need to worry about that just yet. While munching on the last Oreo, he looked up at the endless summer sky and wondered what Callie was doing at that moment. He'd told her he'd be home in the late afternoon if she wanted to leave Henry with him, but she had seemed reluctant. Maybe he'd swing by on his way home and see if she'd changed her mind. It had been so good to see her; and one thing was certain . . . she was as beautiful as ever.

The afternoon passed quickly, and when Linden stopped to look at the clock in the truck, he couldn't believe how late it was. He'd made good progress, but he'd also begun to realize that this job was going to take much longer than he'd expected. He pulled on his shirt, packed up his things, and headed back down through the pasture. As he neared the house, he saw Fairbanks standing outside, wearing different clothes but still having the same careless look of someone whose mind was preoccupied with thoughts more profound than what to wear. His friends had arrived bearing gifts: bottles of wine, baked goods, and a lovely bouquet of lilies. They were all standing in the driveway and, when Fairbanks spied the truck coming down the hill, he waved for Linden to stop and held out a plate of brownies. "These little delights are *not* from a box," he declared with a wink.

Linden smiled and took one. "Thanks! Are you going to Harlow's?" he asked.

"I think so, but we're going to have cocktails first. Care to join us?"

Linden was surprised by the invitation. "No . . . no, thanks," he stammered. He looked over and nodded to two older gentlemen and a pretty, middle-aged woman standing near an old, green Range Rover with New York plates. "I have some things to take care of, but I'll be back tomorrow."

Fairbanks nodded. "Well, you must take another brownie, then."

As Linden pulled away, he glanced in his

rearview mirror and watched Fairbanks and his friends climb the porch steps. It would have been fun to stay, but he really wanted to give Callie the chance to see her dad. He looked at the clock and sighed. He really needed to shower too, but if he took the time to go home, visiting hours might be over.

26

Callie was washing dishes and Henry was sitting in his booster seat finishing supper when Linden knocked on the screen door. They both looked up in surprise.

"Hey!" Callie said, drying her hands. "Come in."

Linden pulled open the door, smiling shyly, and ruffled Henry's hair. "How's my little helper?"

Callie watched the exchange and shook her head. "Your little helper has had another long day with *his* mean mom."

"Naaw," Linden teased, looking at Henry. "Are you giving your mom a hard time again?" Henry slurped in a long string of spaghetti and didn't respond.

Callie shook her head and sighed. "Have you had supper?"

"No, but that's not why I came," he said. "I came so you could run over to see your dad."

"You didn't have to do that," she said,

137

considering the offer. "I might, though, if you'll eat some spaghetti." She motioned to the bowl. "I always make too much."

Linden looked at the mound of spaghetti in the bowl and his stomach rumbled. He patted it with an embarrassed grin. "I guess I can help with that."

"Good!" Callie said. "There's bread and salad, *and* blueberry muffins." She pointed to a plate on the counter.

Linden nodded. "Okay, but you better go."

Callie glanced at the clock and then around the kitchen. "Leave the dishes."

"I will."

"Promise?"

He grinned, and she eyed him. "You better," she said warningly. She grabbed her bag, kissed Henry on the top of the head, and looked at Linden. "Thank you so much. I won't be long."

Linden leaned against the counter and nodded toward the door. "Go."

After Callie left, Linden fixed a plate of spaghetti, sat down next to Henry, and noticed that Henry's cup was empty. "Want more milk?" Henry nodded slightly, and Linden refilled his cup and poured a glass for himself. "I bet Springer and Kat are hungry too," he said, thinking of the animals. Henry looked around at the mention of the two dogs, and Linden shook his head. "They're not here, Henry. I was just thinking of them." He studied the little boy's face and wondered if he always took what was said to him literally. Maybe he should be more careful about what he said.

After supper, he cleared the dishes and, remembering Callie's admonishment, smiled as he turned on the hot water and poured soap onto the sponge. He washed the few dishes, looked out the window at the neglected gardens, and remembered how meticulous they'd once been. He washed Henry's plate and cup, put them in the dish drain, dried his hands, and turned to look at him. "Want to go for a walk?" Henry immediately climbed down and headed for the door.

As they started up the dirt road, Henry slipped his small hand into Linden's and Linden was suddenly reminded of another hand he'd once held while walking on this road. *Who would have thought that, years later, I'd walk here holding her son's hand? Life certainly takes some unexpected turns!* As they continued along, Linden recalled the autumn afternoon when he and Callie had stopped, just out of view of the house. He looked around, trying to get his bearings, and remembered an old majestic maple tree that had showered them with red and orange leaves. He pictured himself as an awkward, skinny fifteen-year-old with a pounding heart . . . and Callie seeming so sure of herself. He had pulled her toward him and she'd just closed her eyes, leaning up to him, and softly kissed him back. He could still taste the sweetness of her lips. . . .

He felt a sudden tug on his hand and looked down. Henry, bored by the delay, had slipped free and begun walking along a rut in the side of the road. Linden caught up to him, and Henry glanced over his shoulder and began to trot. Linden picked up his pace too and teased, "Are we racing?" As soon as he said the words, though, he regretted it, because Henry started to run faster. Linden jogged beside him, feeling his sore muscles protesting. "Wouldn't you rather walk?" he asked, but Henry just kept going, his little legs chugging along. Linden settled into a steady pace beside him and wondered how far Henry could run.

27

It was 7:50 when Callie stopped in front of the nurses' station near the ICU. A nurse looked up, glanced at the clock, and said, "You just made it." Callie smiled and continued on to her dad's room. She peered around his door and saw Dr. Franklin standing beside his bed with a clipboard tucked against his chest.

"Hi," she said softly. Her dad smiled, and Dr. Franklin looked up.

"Hey! You are just the person I wanted to see."

"I am?"

Dr. Franklin slipped a book from behind the

clipboard. "I thought you might like to read this. It's written by a woman who has autism." Callie took the book and looked at the title, *Thinking in Pictures*. Dr. Franklin continued, "Temple Grandin's books have had a tremendous impact on our understanding of autism and, more importantly, on our understanding of how those with autism see and understand the world."

"Thank you," Callie said, taking it and skimming the back cover.

"But that's not the only reason I was hoping to see you." He paused, and Callie looked up. "Your dad and I have just been talking about his new test results. They show that one of his arteries has more blockage than we initially thought." He paused. "So much so that I think it would be best for him to have the surgery sooner, rather than later."

Callie took a deep breath in. "Is he strong enough?"

"He is, and I don't think his strength will improve much more if we don't help his heart."

"Oh," she said, looking at her dad. "How soon?" she asked pensively.

"I was hoping to do it tomorrow."

"Tomorrow?!" Callie felt her heart and head both start to pound at once, and she rubbed her temple.

She reached for her dad's hand, and Dr. Franklin gently reassured her. "Callie, it's a standard operation. I've performed it hundreds of times." He looked at Ben. "And you will feel much better after."

Callie searched her dad's eyes, trying to read how he felt about having surgery so soon. From his smile and nod, though, she could tell he was already resigned to the idea. "There's no sense putting it off, Cal," he said.

Dr. Franklin reached for his pen. "I just need a couple of signatures, then, and we'll plan on first thing in the morning." Callie watched her father's once strong, steady hand shaking as he signed the papers. Dr. Franklin put his hand on Callie's shoulder. "Don't worry, Callie. Everything will be fine." He stopped at the door on his way out, looked back at Ben, and reminded him, "No breakfast." Ben nodded.

There were rare moments in Callie's life when she felt as if God was speaking to her through the counsel of another person and she suddenly realized that this was one of those times. Dr. Franklin's words had swept over her and left her with a sense of peace . . . and, even though she knew she would probably still worry, in the end everything would be fine.

She sat on the edge of her dad's bed and smiled. "Are you okay?"

Ben nodded. "Are you?"

She nodded too. "Remember what Mom used to say?"

"She used to say a lot of things. . . ."

"Well, one thing she said was, 'All will be well . . . and all will be well . . .'"

Ben smiled and joined in, "'. . . and all will be well . . . no matter what.'"

Callie gave him a long hug. "I'll be here."

"You don't need to be."

"Well, I will be," she said firmly.

"You always were stubborn," he teased.

"I got it from *you*," she teased back.

28

The sun was setting when Callie pulled into the driveway of the little ranch. She walked toward the dark house and wondered where Henry and Linden were.

"Linden?" she called.

"Back here."

Callie walked around the house but still couldn't see him.

"Over here," Linden said, standing up and throwing a handful of weeds into a wooden bushel.

"Where's Henry?"

"Right here," he said, pointing down. A little hand reached out and dropped a weed into the bushel.

"You guys are weeding?" she asked incredulously.

Linden grinned. "Well, first, your son took me on a little run and, when we got back, it was too hot inside so we just walked around out here. We saw that the gardens needed weeding, and we found this old bushel in the garage." As he said this, the little fist reached out and dropped in another weed.

Linden smiled. "You have a good little worker."

Callie shook her head. "And *you* have an amazing way with him. I don't know how you do it. He mimics everything you do."

Linden shrugged. "With simple tasks, he's very focused."

Callie laughed. "Probably more than I ever was . . . or will be!"

Linden brushed his hands off and stepped toward her. "How's your dad?"

Callie looked at the streaks of orange along the horizon and realized that the feeling of peace she'd felt at the hospital was waning. She blinked back tears and said, "He's having surgery tomorrow."

Linden saw her eyes glistening in the evening light and, without thinking, wrapped her in a hug. "He's going to be okay, Cal," he whispered.

Callie nodded, and Linden stepped back to make sure she wasn't crying. As he did, he remembered that he still hadn't showered, and he took another step back. Callie looked up, puzzled. "I forgot that I really need a shower," he said.

"You *could* just shower here," she teased mischievously.

"And what would your dad think, since *you* are the only one home?"

"He wouldn't think anything of it. He already knows I'm a lost cause."

Linden searched her eyes and shook his head. "No, you're not," he said quietly.

Callie looked away. She hadn't expected this. She hadn't expected Linden to forgive her so easily. They hadn't even talked about anything yet. Didn't he want to know?

Linden lifted her chin. "Callie, I wish I could stay, *and* take a shower," he added with a smile, "but I'm afraid I have some very hungry animals waiting for me."

Callie suddenly remembered all the animals. "Oh, I forgot!" she exclaimed. "You'd better go!"

Linden nodded. "Why don't I pick Henry up on my way to work tomorrow?"

Callie looked puzzled. "Linden, I don't expect you to watch Henry tomorrow."

"Well, what are you going to do?"

"I don't know," she said, hesitating. "I hadn't gotten that far. Besides, how can you take him to work?" She shook her head in dismay. "I don't even know what you do. How can that be? Have we only talked about *me?*"

"No, we haven't only talked about *you.*" He paused. "Besides, it's not a big deal. I just rebuild old stone walls, and tomorrow I'm working on a farm in Dublin. I'm sure Henry will be fine. Maybe I'll even put him to work. And, if he's not happy, we won't stay."

Callie shook her head. "I don't know. This is crazy. I can't keep asking you to take care of him."

"Why not?"

"Because it's not right."

"Cal, it's sort of an emergency, don't you think?"

She nodded but then shook her head too. "Oh, I just don't know what to do!"

"Then don't even think about it. Is eight too early?"

"Eight is fine." She sighed. "I don't know how I can ever repay you."

Linden grinned. "Spaghetti again would be good. I think there's still plenty." Callie laughed, and Linden smiled. "Hey, at least you're laughing." He looked in Henry's direction. "Bye, Henry." Then he looked at Callie. "Good night," he said with a gentle smile.

"Good night," she replied. "Thank you again."

She watched him pull away and then walked over to where Henry was working. Even in the dark, she could see that he was still methodically pulling grass and weeds from the soft earth. "Henry, *you* are doing a really good job," she said softly.

29

Callie had trouble falling asleep that night. By the time Henry was washed up and in bed, she was exhausted, but worried thoughts about her dad still plagued her mind. Finally, she got up, wandered to the kitchen, opened the fridge, and stared absentmindedly at its contents. The cool air drifted out, and she could hear her dad's voice: "Callie, please don't stand there with the door open. It's not an air conditioner." She smiled, took out the milk, and poured a small glass. Then she turned on the stove light and saw the new batteries on the counter next to the remote control. She pried out the old ones, popped in the new ones, and went into the living room to see if it worked. The TV came right on. *Finally, something that works!*

She was about to turn it off again when she realized that *The Tonight Show* was starting. She sat down on the edge of her dad's favorite chair and watched Jay Leno greeting his audience, and remembered how her parents had always stayed up late to watch Johnny Carson. When she was little, she'd sometimes lain awake, listening to the big band sound of "Johnny's Theme" before drifting off to the comforting sound of her parents' laughter. The memory made her smile. After Jay had taken over, her parents hadn't stayed

147

up as often and, after her mom's accident, her dad hadn't stayed up at all, but Callie still liked to watch it once in a while. When she was away at school, she'd often turned it on to get a break from her homework. She sank back into her dad's comfortable old chair and listened to Jay's monologue. Moments later, she was sound asleep.

The next morning, she woke with a start and realized that *The Tonight Show* had somehow become the *Today* show and her glass of milk was still sitting on the table. She sat up, glanced at the clock, groaned, dumped the milk down the drain, peeked in on Henry, and hopped in the shower. Linden would be there any minute!

She was towel-drying her hair and sifting through a pile of folded laundry, looking for something to wear, when she heard a knock on the door. She groaned again, wrapped the towel around her, and hurried to answer it. Linden was standing outside in the early morning sun.

"Hey!" she said, obviously frazzled. She unhooked the door, pushed it open, and saw that he was holding two cups of Dunkin' Donuts coffee and a box of Munchkins. "Oh, my goodness! *You* are a lifesaver! We are running late. I overslept, and Henry's not even up yet!"

"It's okay, it's not like I have to punch a clock. I can get there anytime or not at all. You are the one that needs to get going."

"I know. . . ." Callie relaxed for one second and smiled. "ButI need to get dressed first."

"I see that," he said with a grin. "Need help?" Callie gave him a funny look, and he laughed. "Just kidding! Go."

A few minutes later, a dressed Callie ushered a cranky Henry across the hall to use the bathroom. When he started to protest, she whispered, "Linden's here and he brought a treat." This bit of news brought immediate cooperation, and Callie just shook her head. "I don't know why you don't act this way for me."

Moments later, Henry appeared shyly in the kitchen doorway and Linden looked up from the book Callie had left on the table. His hair was damp and neatly combed, and he was wearing green shorts and a John Deere T-shirt.

"Here's my little helper," Linden said with a smile.

"I'm coming," Callie hollered from the bathroom. She took one last look in the mirror and sighed. It was the best she could do.

She joined them in the kitchen wearing white shorts and a light blue sleeveless T-shirt. Linden looked at her outfit. "Hmmm, I liked the towel better."

She rolled her eyes and shook her head at the same time.

"You're pretty good at that," he teased.

She grinned. "Would you like to see it again?"

"Sure."

"Well, you'll have to wait."

Linden handed one of the coffees to her, and Callie took it, breathed in its fresh aroma, and sighed, "Thank you." She took a sip and nodded to Henry, and Linden looked over and realized he was gazing longingly at the pink and orange box on the table.

"Do you like Munchkins?" Linden asked. Henry nodded shyly, and Linden said, "Well, you can help yourself." Henry just stood there, and Linden shook his head. "I'm sorry, Henry. What I mean is: 'Come over and pick out the ones you like.'" He held the box out, and Henry peered inside and carefully took out one chocolate and one coconut. "You're a man after my own heart," he said, but as soon as he said it, he knew it probably didn't make any sense to Henry either. He looked back at Callie. "Do you have to be careful how you word things?"

"What do you mean?" she asked.

"Well, I've noticed Henry seems to take everything literally. Last night, I said Kat and Springer were probably hungry, and he looked around the kitchen to see if they were here." At these words, Henry glanced around the kitchen again, and Linden shook his head. "Henry, Kat and Springer are *not* here." He looked back at Callie. "Did you notice, a moment ago, when I said he could help himself to Munchkins, he didn't move, but when I said he could pick out the

150

ones he likes, he came right over?" Linden looked at Henry. "If you think about it, Cal, the phrase 'you can help yourself' *is* sort of abstract."

Callie nodded. "I guess I never really paid attention."

Linden smiled. "Well, how do you *pay* attention? Do you give him a check?"

"I see what you mean. It's as if he only understands exact meaning."

"It's just an observation," Linden said. He nodded toward the book. "This book looks interesting. Is that what Henry has? Autism?"

"The doctor seems to think so, but I haven't had a chance to find out very much about it. I only have the brochures she gave me, and Dr. Franklin gave that book to me last night." She glanced at the clock on the stove. "I should go."

Linden nodded and stood up. "Yup, we're going too." He looked at Henry and held out the box of Munchkins. "Can you carry these?" Henry took the box, and Callie picked up the book, slipped it into her bag, and slung the bag over her shoulder. Then she balanced her cup of coffee in her other hand and started to push open the door, but stopped. "I forgot to make a lunch for Henry!"

"Don't worry, I have plenty."

"Are you sure? Do you want to take some muffins?"

Linden shook his head. "No, but you should. I'm sure you haven't eaten anything."

"I'm fine," she replied. "I have coffee. That's all I need."

"Okay, well, make sure you tell your dad I'm praying for him."

Callie smiled. "I will." But then she stopped again. "You need the car seat."

They went outside and Linden lifted the car seat into the truck, and Callie showed him how to secure it. "You are definitely getting a crash course in parenting," she said as Linden helped Henry climb in. "I'll pick him up as soon as I can." She studied Linden's face. "I hope everything goes okay, and I hope he's no trouble." She kissed Henry's cheek and whispered, "Be good." Henry was contentedly munching another Munchkin, though, and swinging his feet at the same time, so she couldn't tell if he nodded.

As she walked to her car, she looked back. "Don't forget that he takes off."

"I won't forget."

Callie waved and, as she drove away, prayed they'd be okay.

Twenty minutes later she was hurrying down the hospital corridor, feeling as if she lived there. She stopped in front of the nurses' station. Jess looked up and smiled. "They just wheeled your daddy into surgery. Dr. Franklin is the best. Everything's going to be just fine."

Callie's heart sank. "Is it too late to see him?"

Jess nodded. "I'm afraid so, honey. But he'll be done in a couple of hours, although he might not be awake that soon."

Callie felt like kicking herself. *How can I be late today, of all days? How did I miss letting him know I was there? Why am I always such a screwup?* Tears filled her eyes as she went to find a quiet place to wait. *Oh, Dad, I'm so sorry I missed you. Please know I'm here. . . .*

30

As the morning passed, Linden worked steadily. Henry watched him and then began a project of his own. Linden looked over to see what he was up to and realized he was building a miniature wall. He shook his head, amazed that this quiet little boy was able to contentedly entertain himself with a pastime most kids would find boring. He walked over to take a closer look. "Hey, that looks great."

Henry nodded and continued to pile the small stones.

"Hellooo!" a friendly voice called. Linden turned and saw Fairbanks coming up the hill.

"Good morning!"

"Good morning to you! It's going to be another hot one." Henry glanced up and then shyly looked away. Fairbanks smiled. "Who's this little fellow?"

"This is Henry," Linden replied. "Henry, this is Mr. Thompson."

"Nice to meet you, Henry. Please, though, call me Fairbanks. Everyone does." Henry glanced sideways and then quickly looked away again, and Fairbanks gave Linden a puzzled look.

"You'll have to excuse Henry," he said. "He's a man of few . . . actually *no* words."

Fairbanks leaned against the wall, took off his glasses, wiped his brow with a handkerchief that he pulled from his back pocket, and crossed his arms. "I was once a man of few words." He paused thoughtfully. "No words at all?"

Linden shook his head. "He nods sometimes, but mostly he likes to give his mom a hard time, tantrums and such."

Fairbanks nodded thoughtfully. "Maybe that's his only way of communicating. I struggled with the same thing when I was a youngster. I wasn't able to vocalize the way I was feeling. It was very frustrating for me *and* my parents. In fact, it's only by the grace of God and my mother's love and patience that I didn't end up in an institution. That's what people did with kids with autism back then. Regular folks just couldn't understand our world. Most still don't."

"*You* had autism?" Linden sounded incredulous.

Fairbanks glanced sideways and smiled mischievously. "I still do."

"But you've had so much success. I never would have guessed . . ."

Fairbanks wiped his glasses on his shirt. "I

wasn't always 'a success,' as you call it. I struggled tremendously. We all do." He watched Henry working intently. "I bet Henry's mom will eventually discover that he's good at a great many things. She just needs to be patient and help him figure out what they are." He knelt down next to Henry and gently touched his arm. Henry looked up and Fairbanks smiled. "*That* is a very nice stone wall, Henry." Henry nodded and continued to work, his brow furrowed in concentration.

Fairbanks looked back at Linden. "Do sounds bother him?"

Linden shook his head. "I don't know."

"Children with autism are usually very sensitive to light and sound. Stop at the house on your way home. I may have something that will help." With that, he stood. "Well, I'm off for a hike. Hopefully it will get the creative juices flowing!" He looked back and waved and Henry, who was watching him go, made a slight gesture with his hand. Linden raised his eyebrows in surprise.

After Fairbanks had gone, Linden lifted his cooler out of the truck and looked over at Henry. "Ready for lunch?" Henry got up and trundled over to see what *was* for lunch, and Linden took out a peanut butter and jelly sandwich, unwrapped it, and handed him half. Henry took a big bite and sat down on the grass, but when Linden found a seat on a nearby rock, Henry got up and sat down near him. Linden leaned forward with his elbows on his knees while he ate and looked out across the pasture. Henry watched him out of the corner of his eye and then leaned forward too, resting his tan arms on his small round knees. Linden smiled, unwrapped another sandwich, and held out another half. Henry stood up, took it, and sat back down.

Late in the afternoon, Linden pulled up in front of the old white farmhouse and Fairbanks came to the door wearing a green headset over his ears. "My father was a pilot!" he explained loudly. "When I was little, he figured out that I didn't like noise, so one day, he brought these home." Fairbanks reached up and touched where the wires had been cut off and continued loudly, "I wore them when we went to restaurants." He smiled. "Everyone gave us funny looks, but my parents didn't care." He took the headset off and continued to explain in the same loud voice but then realized he was speaking too loudly. In a softer voice he continued, "My parents were just happy because I was better able to tolerate outings and they enjoyed going out to dinner." He looked at Henry. "If noise bothers him, they might prove helpful. You can have them. I haven't used them in years."

"Thanks," Linden said. "I'll pass them along to his mom."

"I forgot all about them until I started writing

this memoir. I've been thinking back, trying to explain how I, as a boy, perceived the world and how I learned to live in it."

Linden nodded thoughtfully. "I'd like to read it someday."

Fairbanks smiled, took off his glasses, and wiped them on his shirt. He suddenly looked a bit distracted. "Someday . . ." he murmured.

Linden put the headset on his head and climbed in the truck. Henry looked at him curiously, furrowed his brow, and then looked away, but when Linden took the headset off and reached over to put them on Henry, he didn't resist.

Linden looked back at Fairbanks, raised his eyebrows and shrugged.

Fairbanks nodded. "We sometimes mimic what people do. That's how we get our clues." Linden listened to Fairbanks refer to himself and others who have autism as "we," almost as if they were a separate class of people. It sounded odd.

"Thank you again," Linden said as he started the truck. He began to pull away but then stopped to call back. "I may not be here the next couple of days. I have a cow that's about to calve, and I need to keep an eye on her."

Fairbanks nodded and waved. "No hurry!"

31

Callie had been sitting in the waiting room, staring at the same print for what seemed like hours. She had noticed it as soon as she sat down, and she'd immediately stood back up to walk over and look at the title. The gold plate read, A VIEW OF THE MOUNTAIN PASS CALLED THE NOTCH OF THE WHITE MOUNTAINS, 1839. Below the title was the name of the artist: THOMAS COLE (1801–1848). *It doesn't look like Franconia,* she thought, *so it must be Crawford.* She took a sip of her coffee and did the math: Thomas Cole was only thirty-eight when he painted it and he died nine years later. She wondered why he had died so young. She opened the book on her lap and tried to read but soon found herself gazing at the painting again.

It was beautiful. The sun-dappled trees were swept with red and orange brushstrokes, and although it seemed like a tranquil autumn scene at first, the viewer soon realized that a storm was imminent. To the west, a threatening cloud, bursting with rain, was coming over the mountain, and a man on a black horse was racing through the pass, trying to reach the safety of a white house tucked at the base of the mountain. The clear blue autumn sky and sun-filled valley were contrasted ominously against the black clouds and shadows of the storm sweeping over the mountain. Callie gazed at it, her eyes taking in every detail. She felt the urgency the painter was trying to express and she understood all too well the feeling of racing, running, and longing for safety.

Callie's mind wandered back to the art history class she'd taken in college. She'd dreaded that class! Slide after slide flashing across a tremendous screen in an impersonal lecture hall while the art professor droned on and on. Callie had tried to remember each artist and date by finding a part of the painting that looked like a letter or number to trigger a clue, but it had all seemed so pointless. What mattered in art was how the painting made you feel. She sighed. So few of those paintings made her feel the way this one did. It was how she felt all the time!

She looked at the clock. It was twelve-thirty. She took a sip of her now cold coffee and wondered if there was a microwave nearby. Maybe she should get something to eat too, although she still wasn't very hungry. Her stomach was too tied up in knots of worry. She stood to stretch her legs, stepped closer to the painting, and thought of the time she and her parents had hiked from Crawford Notch to Ethan Pond. It had been on her tenth birthday and, when they finally got there, she'd been so hot she'd jumped in the pond with all her clothes on. Somewhere in the house there was a picture of her standing next to her dad, wet and grinning. *Oh, how I'd love to go back to the carefree simplicity of that day,* she thought longingly.

Callie turned from the painting and went to look for a microwave. As she rounded the corner, she saw Jess standing outside one of the rooms, looking at the open notebook on her medicine cart. "Hey, Jess," Callie said.

Jess looked up and smiled. "Hey, honey, any news yet?" Callie shook her head and Jess looked at her watch. "Anytime, now, don't you worry. Dr. Franklin is the best."

Callie nodded. "Do you guys have a place I can nuke this?" she asked, holding up her coffee cup.

"I can do better than that. There's a fresh pot in that little room right there, and there's a plate of homemade brownies one of the nurses brought in. Help yourself."

"Thanks."

"Have you eaten anything today?"

Callie shook her head.

"Do you want somethin' more than brownies? They're goin' 'round with the food cart and there's always extra. It's not your typical hospital food either. Not like when your mama worked here. It's all fresh local produce and everythin'. You should try it."

"Thanks, but I'm not very hungry."

"You should eat, girl! You're too skinny! You need to put some meat on those bones." She patted her own round arm. "Have one of those brownies. They are yum-*mee!*"

"Okay, I will." Callie disappeared into the nurses' room. She warmed up the little bit of coffee left in her cup with some from the fresh pot and then took a small brownie and retreated to the waiting area. A middle-aged couple and a doctor were standing in the hall, talking quietly. The woman was crying and the man had his arm around her shoulders. Callie looked at the painting and tried not to eavesdrop, but she quickly realized that the couple's teenage son had just been diagnosed with cancer. Listening to their hushed anguish, Callie's eyes filled with tears. *Oh, God, why do You let these things happen? What lesson can his parents learn from this . . . besides grief and despair?*

Out of the blue an answer filled Callie's mind. *They can learn to trust me!* Callie shook her head in wonder and glanced at the couple. The woman's sobbing was easing, and the man was nodding resolutely. Callie could tell, from the change in their demeanor, that they were not giving up. They were determined to win this fight and, like it or not, they *would* learn to trust. She looked at the painting again and wondered if the man on the horse ever reached the safety of the house. It was a question that the artist had purposely left unanswered.

Callie reached for the book beside her and

thought of Henry and Linden. She closed her eyes and prayed that everyone she loved would be okay. What more could she do? She needed to learn to trust too and she wondered if this was *her* lesson.

Moments later, Dr. Franklin appeared, and Callie stood up, her heart pounding. He smiled. "Everything went well. Your dad's in recovery. He's still a bit groggy, but you can see him."

A ray of sunshine spilled into the corner of her dad's room as Callie sat near his bed and watched his chest rise and fall. He was sound asleep . . . but he was alive and his prognosis was good. She held his hand and whispered a prayer of thanksgiving.

32

Henry traipsed along after Linden, still wearing the pilot's headset. Behind him trailed Springer, and moseying along on her own was Kat. Henry had helped Linden feed the animals, but Linden had quickly discovered that, with the headset on, Henry didn't hear anything and he'd had to motion with his hands to communicate with him. He'd begun to wonder if the headset was a bad idea. He hoped Callie wouldn't be upset about it and, if she didn't approve, he hoped Henry didn't give her a hard time. He suddenly had a funny feeling about the whole thing, which was never a good sign.

Callie raised her eyebrows when she saw the oversized headphones covering her son's ears and Linden quickly explained. "It turns out Fairbanks has autism too, but you'd never know it . . . except for a couple of quirky little things he does." Callie listened as Linden went on. "Why don't we give 'em a try? Fairbanks said he used to wear them when he was little. It made it easier for his parents to go out to dinner, and you said Henry wasn't fond of restaurants, so I thought we could go to Harlow's tonight and see if it helps."

"I don't know," Callie said slowly. "What if they don't help? Besides, I thought you wanted spaghetti."

"We can have spaghetti another time, and if Henry's not happy, we'll get dinner to go."

Callie hesitated. "All right," she said finally.

"I just need to take a quick shower," Linden said.

"Need help?" Callie teased. Linden raised his eyebrows, and she laughed, suddenly embarrassed. "Just kidding."

"Want a beer?" Linden called as he went inside.

"No, thanks, but I'll have a sip of yours."

"*Mine* will be in the shower with me."

"Oh, well, save some for me, then." She sank into one of the chairs on the porch and watched Henry gently stroking Springer's soft ears. As she watched, she realized that her son seemed to be teasing the hapless dog. He'd pet him and then take his hand away, and moments later Springer would open his eyes and nuzzle Henry's hand for more and Henry would oblige briefly but stop again, waiting for Springer to nudge him again.

A few minutes later, Linden pushed open the screen door. His hair was wet and he was wearing a clean white T-shirt with a picture of Tuckerman's Ravine on the back. He held his beer out to Callie, and she took it and nodded toward Henry. "Watch what my son is doing to your poor dog." Linden watched Henry pet Springer and then stop and wait for his hand to be nudged.

Linden grinned. "He's just like his mother . . . a big tease!"

Callie laughed and took a sip of the beer. "Mmmm, this tastes good." She handed it back to him. "Are you ready, finally?"

"Yup."

Linden pulled the car seat out of the truck and put it back in Callie's car.

"I can't believe you're still driving this Nova," he said.

"Two hundred twenty-eight thousand miles!" she said proudly.

"No!"

"Yup!" she said, beaming.

Linden helped Henry climb in and then pulled the seat back and got in too. He shook his head and looked around. "Lots of memories in this old car," he said wistfully. Callie smiled, remembering too.

Even though it was early, Harlow's Pub was busy. Henry trundled through the crowded restaurant, wearing the headset and holding Linden's hand. A friendly waitress showed them to a table in back, eyed Henry curiously, took their drink order, and disappeared. Linden turned Henry's paper place mat over and, with a pen he pulled from his pocket, drew a quick sketch of a cartoonish dog that looked a lot like Springer. Henry reached for the pen and immediately began drawing what looked like a small person standing beside the dog.

"Do you know what you're having?" Callie asked, peering over the top of her menu. "We should try to make this quick."

Linden nodded. "Just waiting on you."

"You already know?" she asked in surprise.

"Yup."

Callie looked back at the menu as the waitress returned with their drinks. "Ready to order?" she asked. Henry continued to draw and didn't look up.

Callie smiled. "I think so. . . ." She looked at Linden. "Go ahead."

Linden handed the waitress his unopened menu. "I'll have a Reuben, please."

Callie smiled, still studying the menu and feeling the pressure of the waitress's eyes. "Hmmm . . . how 'bout an Avocado Bliss and a BLT for Henry," she said, closing the menu and handing it to her with a smile. "Thank you."

Callie watched Henry drawing contentedly on the place mat and sighed. "I don't know if it's the headset, the pen, or *you,* but it's never this easy."

"It's me," Linden said with a grin.

Callie took a sip of her drink and shook her head.

"So, the surgery went well and your dad woke up right before you left?"

She nodded again.

"What happens next?"

"I'm not sure. Rehab, I guess." She sighed. "I just wish he were strong enough to move back home."

"Maybe he will be. My uncle had stents put in after his heart attack, and he felt much better. He had to change his lifestyle though. Exercise and diet . . . and my aunt had to keep after him all the time."

Callie nodded. "Well, I hope they move him out of ICU soon so Henry can see him. I think that'll cheer him up."

"Are you going tomorrow?"

Callie shook her head in dismay and laughed. "I don't know. Are you free?"

"I'll be around all day. Reba is going to have her calf soon and I need to keep an eye on her, but if she seems okay in the morning, I thought maybe we could go for a hike."

The waitress brought over a tray with their

sandwiches and asked if they needed anything else. They both shook their heads and she disappeared again.

"Where are you thinking of hiking?"

"Monadnock?" Linden replied questioningly, taking a bite of his sandwich.

"Don't you think that's a little far for Henry?"

Linden shook his head, swallowed. "I think there's one of those L.L.Bean child carriers in the attic."

Callie took a bite of her sandwich and nodded thoughtfully. "Oh, my goodness, this sandwich is amazing," she said, her mouth full. "I love avocado. Do you want to try it?"

Linden laughed. "No, thanks, I believe you. But somehow you've managed to get some of that amazing avocado on your chin."

Callie found the avocado with her finger and licked it. "Thank you," she said with a grin. She looked over at Henry and realized he was still drawing. "Henry," she called, trying to get his attention, but he didn't hear her. Linden touched Henry's arm and pushed the plate toward him, inadvertently covering his drawing.

Clutching the pen in his fist, Henry angrily pushed the plate away and almost spilled his milk. "Hey!" Linden said in surprise.

"Leave him," Callie said quietly. "If he gets upset, we'll have to leave. I'll just have it wrapped and he can eat it later."

"How do you know when he's just being defiant?" Linden asked.

"I don't," she replied, shaking her head. "That's the hard part."

Callie drove slowly along the dirt road leading to the cabin. When she pulled in, several sets of startled eyes looked up, glowing mischievously. "Damn those raccoons!" Linden growled. He opened his door, and the raccoons scurried off in the direction of the river, bickering as they went, but the damage was already done: the birdfeeder was on the ground and the seed that was left was scattered across the ground.

"You have all kinds of wildlife out here," Callie teased.

Linden nodded. "And *some* are not welcome!" He peered into the backseat and realized Henry was sound asleep. "Want to come in?"

Callie looked in back too. "No, I better not. I'm sure I'll have my own battle to wage when I get home."

"I wish it were easier for you," Linden said sympathetically.

"Sometimes I think it's my punishment." She smiled sadly, hoping Linden caught on to what she was trying to say, but he just looked puzzled.

"Thanks for dinner. It was fun."

Callie nodded. "It was really nice. Thank *you* for the idea."

"You can drop Henry off as early as you'd like tomorrow, and when you get back we'll decide about hiking."

"Okay. 'Night."

" 'Night." Linden closed the car door, pushed his hands into his pockets, and watched as the Nova's taillights slowly disappeared into the darkness. Then he picked up the battered, empty birdfeeder and leaned it against the corner of the porch. He opened the screen door and the dogs bounded past him off the porch, eager to track the interlopers. Linden watched them for a few minutes and then smelled another strong scent drifting through the air. "C'mon, you two! In!" The dogs took care of business and then reluctantly padded up the steps . . . just as a ball of black and white fur waddled around the corner of the house.

Linden wandered into the room off the kitchen, turned the light on over his drawing table, and studied his painting. He reached for a brush, gently slapped the dust from it, and then squeezed some fresh colors onto his palette. He swished the brush into the water jar and began to wet the paper with it. While he worked, he thought about Henry . . . and later, before he went to bed, he dug out an old sketch pad and pencil set for him.

33

It seemed that the absence of sunlight overnight had done little to fend off the oppressive heat wave that rolled back in at dawn. Callie listened to the weatherman as she made coffee. "One more day of this heat and then we'll have some storms roll through tomorrow afternoon and hopefully push it out of here. Some storms will be severe, though, so keep an eye on the sky. Once they pass, we're setting up for a nice weekend: sunny and low humidity with temps in the eighties."

"Thank goodness!" Callie murmured. It was almost too hot to drink coffee. *One cup, just to get going,* she thought, *and the rest is going in the fridge for iced coffee.* She clicked the coffee-maker off as soon as it was done brewing, poured steaming coffee into the U.S. Navy mug, and took the mug down the hall with her to take a quick shower.

A half hour later, Henry was sitting at the table, devouring his second blueberry muffin, and Callie was packing the rest of them to take to Linden's. She took the last one out of the microwave, broke it open, smoothed butter between the two halves, leaned against the counter, and took a bite. It practically melted in her mouth.

To her dismay, Henry had slid the headset over his ears as soon as she'd finished combing his hair. It had been a struggle to get him to take them off the night before, but he'd finally agreed and let Travelin' Bear wear them to bed. The poor bear's head had been sandwiched so much that only his nose was visible. Callie had become increasingly skeptical of the idea. She needed Henry to communicate, not shut the world out. And although the headset might help in certain situations, he definitely couldn't wear them all the time.

He was still wearing them, though, when they got to the cabin and she had to gingerly lift the v-belt up around them to get it over his head. Linden scooped Henry up. "Here's my helper," he said, pulling one headphone away from Henry's ear as he spoke, but Henry furrowed his brow and immediately pushed it back. "Hmmm," Linden surmised. "Maybe this wasn't such a good idea."

Callie nodded. "Maybe you could *lose* them today," she said hopefully.

"We'll work on it."

"How's Reba?"

Linden pointed to a shady corner of the meadow. Both cows and the little mule were munching contentedly, but Reba's sides were visibly swollen. "She seems okay," Linden said. "I called Cindy this morning, and she said that the earliest she can get here is tomorrow so, hopefully, Reba will wait."

"Are you still thinking of going for a hike?"

"Sure . . . if you think it's not too hot. I found the child carrier."

"Well, do you want me to pick up grinders on my way back and we'll have a picnic?" She suddenly remembered the muffins and reached back into the car for the container.

Linden lifted off the top and peered inside. "Hmmm, we'll have no trouble with these, will we, Henry?" But Henry was too busy saying hello to the dogs, and couldn't hear him anyway. Linden shook his head and turned his attention back to Callie. "Grinders sound good."

"What kind would you like?"

"You know me. I'm happy with ham and Swiss, lettuce, tomato, mustard, and mayo."

"Still?" she teased, remembering that had been Linden's staple lunch when they were in high school.

"It's better than PB and J every day."

"Hey, that was my dad's specialty," Callie said, pretending to be offended.

"Did you ever think of making your own lunch?"

"No, my dad always added a special ingredient."

Linden looked puzzled. "And what was that?"

"Love."

Linden grinned. "Oh, so what you had was really a PBJ and L sandwich," he teased.

"Yup," Callie said, laughing.

Linden laughed too. "Well, add L to my sandwich too."

"I will, but I don't know if the deli person's L is as good as my dad's."

After Callie pulled away, Linden called the dogs and Henry unwittingly traipsed along after them. He climbed the porch steps and immediately noticed the pad of paper and pencils Linden had found for him. He sat down at the table and Linden squatted down next to him and opened the pencil case; but when Henry reached for one, Linden put his hand over the case. Henry looked up and Linden motioned for him to take the headset off. At first, Henry furrowed his brow, but then slipped the headset off and put it on the table. Linden put the pencil case on the table too, and Henry picked one up and began to draw. While he was drawing, Linden took the muffins and headset inside and then came back out and sat in one of the chairs with his own pad and pencil.

34

Ben Wyeth was sitting up, watching the news, and having breakfast when Callie peered around his door. "Wow! You must be feeling better!"

Ben smiled. "There you are," he said with a smile. He looked around for Henry. "Where's the little guy?"

"Dad, you're still in ICU, so he's still with Linden."

"Oh, right, I forgot. How is he?"

"Which one?" Callie asked, sitting on the edge of his bed.

"Both," Ben answered, trying to push his breakfast tray to the side.

"Are you finished eating?" Callie asked, helping him.

"Except for this," he answered, holding up his coffee cup. "Want some?"

"No, thanks. I'm all set." Callie studied her dad's face and noticed that his color was much better than she'd seen in a long time. "They're fine. Henry's still not talking, but he loves spending time with Linden and his animals, especially his dogs. When Henry's there, they are inseparable, and Linden thinks Henry wants to take them home with him." She grinned. "I think he's right."

Ben nodded thoughtfully. "I'm still concerned about him not talking, though, Cal. You should get in touch with Asa Coleman's wife, Maddie, at the elementary school. She's always been wonderful with the special ed kids, and I'm sure she's had kids like Henry . . . not that he's special ed. But her brother Tim has Down's syndrome. That's what inspired her to start working with them."

Callie nodded. "I will."

Ben smiled. "And, how's Linden? Has he forgiven you yet?"

Callie shook her head. "I don't know, Dad. We haven't even talked about it. He doesn't ask any questions about Henry's father. At the same time, he's so good with Henry, and Henry mimics everything he does. He's like a little shadow, and he definitely cooperates with Linden better than he does with me." She shook her head. "Maybe he senses that Linden is more easygoing than I am. I don't know. I can't quite figure it out."

Ben nodded. "Linden's a good guy, Cal. He's nothing like his high-strung mother."

"That's a polite description," Callie teased, remembering how Linden's demanding and overbearing mother had stood, looking at them with her hands on her hips.

Ben laughed. "I know. I'm trying to be good!"

"Linden wants to go for a hike this afternoon, so maybe we'll get a chance to talk."

Ben nodded. "It sounds like he's good for Henry, and I know he's good for you. Don't let him go, Cal. I need to know there's someone to take care of you two."

"You need someone to take care of *you* too," Callie said. "And I'm hoping you'll be able to come home soon."

Ben put his head back on his pillow. "That'd be nice. . . ."

They were both quiet, lost in their own thoughts, and then Ben took Callie's hand. "You should go. Those boys are waiting for you."

Callie squeezed his hand. "I know, but I'll be back tomorrow." Ben held out his empty coffee cup, and Callie put it on the tray for him and gave him a hug. "Love you," she whispered.

"I love you too, kiddo, more than you'll ever know!"

Callie pulled into Linden's driveway and the self-appointed welcoming committee bounded off the porch to greet her. "Yes! I have food!" she said, laughing, as Springer tried to climb over her, sniffing and wiggling.

"Springer," Linden called. "Hop out of there." Springer backed clumsily out of the car, still wagging his tail hopefully and still working the air with his nose. Linden shook his head. "*You* are completely hopeless!"

"I know," Callie said, "I can't help it."

Linden laughed. "I wasn't talking about . . ."

Callie grinned. ". . . me? I am, though."

"I don't think I'd go that far," Linden teased.

Callie smiled and looked away. "So, are you guys ready?"

"We are. But you need to see something first."

Callie gave him a puzzled look, and Linden motioned for her to follow him. They climbed the porch steps, and Callie immediately noticed that Henry wasn't wearing the headset.

"How'd you get him to take them off?" she whispered.

Linden smiled. "That's not it. Look." He pointed to Henry's paper, and Callie looked over his shoulder. The page was full of drawings, and although they were simple, Callie could tell right away that they were all of Linden's animals. There were two cows, one fatter than the other; two cats, one colored in, one lighter; a mule; two dogs; lots of chickens; and an owl peering down from a tree.

"Wow! Henry, that's beautiful!" Henry looked up and seemed to beam. It was a look Callie had never seen before, and her eyes filled with tears. She looked at Linden. "Those are really good for a three-year-old."

Linden nodded. "They're really good for an *any*-year-old."

Henry looked back down at his paper and continued to draw. This time he concentrated on a small person that looked similar to the one he'd drawn on the paper place mat the night before. This time, however, he placed the person right in the middle of all the animals, but closest to the dogs.

Callie shook her head in disbelief. Henry had always had access to crayons and coloring books at home, but she'd never seen him draw anything on his own before. She glanced over at another pad that had been left open on one of the chairs. She moved around to look at it. "Hey, this is pretty good too," she exclaimed. Linden smiled and shrugged, and Callie picked it up. "It looks *just* like him."

"You can have it," Linden said.

Callie looked up in surprise. "Really?"

Linden nodded and looked down at Henry. "Henry, are you ready to go for a hike?" Henry put the pencil down and stood up, and Linden remarked, "I guess you are!" Callie just shook her head in amazement.

35

In the parking lot of Harling Trail at the base of Mount Monadnock, Henry resisted the child carrier. "Let's just let him walk till he's tired," Callie suggested.

Linden slung the empty carrier onto his shoulders, and looked at the backpack that held their lunch. "Would you rather I carry the lunch pack?"

"I've got it," Callie replied. "It's not heavy."

"You'd say that even if it was."

Callie grinned. "Well, if we happen to get separated, at least I'll have food."

"Always looking out for number one," Linden teased.

"Hey, someone has to," Callie said with a grin.

They started walking along an old logging road with Henry and the two dogs leading the way. Henry pointed to a small pile of rocks, and Linden knelt down to explain. "That's a cairn, Henry. It marks the way to go when there's no place for a painted marker. And, when we come back, it shows us the way we came so we can find our way home. Usually cairns are above the tree line *and* you can always see the next one, unless, of course, you happen to be standing in a cloud." Linden pointed ahead. "See, there's the next one." Henry nodded, picked up a rock, added it to the pile, and trotted ahead. As they continued, he looked for every cairn and, when they reached it, he added a rock.

After about a half mile, they crossed an old stone wall and Linden looked over his shoulder. "Did you know Merino sheep used to graze on this mountain?" Callie shook her head, and Linden continued. "That's why there are stone walls everywhere. A long time ago, farmers purposely burned the forest to create grazing on the upper slopes; some say that's why the mountain is still barren in some areas." The trail began to climb through the forest, and before long, Henry was lagging behind with Springer nosing along beside him. "Are you ready to ride?" Linden asked, setting the carrier down in front of him. Henry furrowed his brow and ran his finger over the nylon fabric that wrapped around the frame. "If you don't like it, you can get out," Linden assured him. Henry put both hands on the frame and lifted his foot, but Linden picked him up before the carrier could fall over and Henry slipped his legs through. Callie tightened the straps snugly over his shoulders and helped Linden lift it onto his back.

"Good thing he's small," he said, tightening the belt around his waist so that most of the weight rested on his hips.

"Are you sure he's not too heavy?"

"Yup," Linden said, hitching the carrier up and tightening the belt again.

They hiked along the path with the dogs gleefully charging ahead, noses to the ground, and going through the motion of leaving their mark even though their tanks were empty. Absent-mindedly, Callie trudged along in Linden's footsteps, watching the easy manner in which he bore Henry's weight.

When they finally hiked out of the low, scraggly undergrowth and out into the sunshine above the tree line, Linden spied another stone cairn and pointed to it. Callie stopped beside him and looked up at Henry. His head was nodding to one side, and she smiled. "I don't think he cares," she said softly.

"Is he asleep?"

Callie nodded and shifted her pack. She could feel her shirt sticking to her back. "I wish this heat would break," she said with a sigh.

"Want to stop?"

"No, we're almost there."

Linden turned and climbed up across the rocks as a warm breeze whispered around them. When they finally reached the uppermost rock outcropping at the summit, they stood side by side, looking north toward the White Mountains. The sky was a hazy blue, not clear and endless like the last time they'd stood there together, but it was still breathtaking. She helped Linden slip the child carrier off his shoulders and set it gently on the ground. Henry stirred and frowned, but didn't wake up . . . and even slept through Springer clumsily stuffing his wet nose in his ear.

Callie opened the backpack and pulled out an empty plastic bowl, and Linden poured water into it. The dogs hurried over, wagging their tails, and lapped it up thirstily. Callie sat down on the sun-drenched rocks, peeled her shirt away from her back, closed her eyes, and smiled.

"Tired?" Linden asked.

"A good tired," she replied. He handed the water bottle to her, and she took a long drink.

"Ready for lunch?"

"Mmmm . . ." she murmured.

He reached into the pack and pulled out the grinders. "Whose is whose?"

"Yours is the one with the L in it," she teased.

"Cute."

"Actually, they're both the same. When Henry wakes up, he can have some of mine."

Linden sat down, handed one of the sandwiches to her, and unwrapped the other one. Springer and Kat immediately looked up from their exploration, sniffed the air, and trotted over to plop down in front of them. "Oh, no, you don't,"

Linden said warningly, "you guys are not sitting there while we have lunch." He reached into the backpack, pulled out two dog biscuits, and moved the dogs about ten feet away. He gave them each their treat and eyed them warily. "Stay." Ever hopeful, the dogs still thumped their tails, and soon Springer had a long string of drool hanging from his jowls. Linden just shook his head and took a bite of his sandwich. Then he glanced over at Henry and said, "I think we should wake him."

Callie nodded. "We will, in a bit. It's nice to just sit and not worry about where he is or what he's into." A warm breeze whispered across the mountain and fluttered the back of her damp shirt. It felt good, and she took another long drink. As she unwrapped her sandwich, she watched Henry too. "He's so easy when he's sleeping."

Linden laughed. "Aren't all kids?"

Callie smiled. "I guess so. I just wish Henry were more like *all* kids. It breaks my heart to think that he'll never lead a normal life, that he'll always be different, and that I'll never even be able to cheer for him from the sidelines." She paused thoughtfully. "Sometimes I can't help but wonder if God is punishing me."

Linden looked up and studied her face. "Cal, you've said that before and I'm not sure what you mean, but I don't think God works that way. *And,* from what you say, I'm not sure who you feel sorrier for, Henry or yourself."

Callie frowned. "I don't feel sorry for myself."

"Well, it sounds like it when you say, '*I* won't ever be able to cheer for him.'"

Callie thought about Linden's words. "I will miss cheering for him and I am sad that he'll miss out on the fun of being on a team, and being cheered for."

Linden gave her his famous half smile. "I know *you* have always thrived on competition. It's part of your personality. In fact, I don't think I've ever met anyone who loves winning more than you do! And I can certainly understand why you would want the same thrilling experience for Henry, but his life will be full of triumphs and joy too, all of his own making. And he will make his mom proud . . . in his own way." Linden looked at the sweet face of the boy sleeping in the child carrier. "And another thing, I honestly don't think God works that way. No matter what wrong we may have done in our lives, God doesn't make bad things happen. Just wait and see, Callie. Henry's life will be full of blessings!"

Callie quietly considered Linden's counsel. It was true: up until now, her heart had ached only for the things she thought Henry wouldn't be able to do. She hadn't begun to dream about what he might achieve.

Linden looked at Henry and recalled how his parents had driven him to succeed. Looking back, he knew it had been all about competition and image. "In a way, Callie, you're lucky. I think parents today are too consumed with the successes of their offspring. The important things in life are not how many goals you score . . . except maybe in *your* case," he teased, "or where you go to college. The important things are about making the most of every moment and making a difference in lives other than your own." He shook his head. "My mom couldn't wait to put that *Dartmouth* decal on the back of her Volvo, right above my brother's *Harvard*. For her, it was all about having successful children for everyone to admire and envy. It absolutely killed her when I didn't finish school." He looked at Callie. "Promise me you won't be that kind of mom."

Callie shook her head. "I won't be."

"I don't know," he teased, "you *are* pretty driven. Remember what you did to your windshield?"

Callie laughed. "Yeah, well, we shouldn't've lost that game."

"But you still don't punch a windshield!"

"You're right," she agreed with a smile. "But I've mellowed since then, and I'm still paying for that mistake. That windshield still leaks."

Linden laughed. "See?" He broke the last piece of his grinder in half and tossed the two pieces to Kat and Springer. They swallowed without even chewing and then gave their undivided attention to Callie.

Linden stood up and stretched his arms over his

head. As he did, his shirt pulled up, and Callie noticed the smooth, tan skin above his boxers. She noticed too that he still didn't wear a belt, and didn't need to. His faded cargo shorts hung comfortably from his slender hips right where they belonged. He turned around and caught her looking, and she quickly glanced away, embarrassed. "I didn't know you didn't finish college," she said quietly.

Linden shrugged. "After we broke up, everything changed." He paused. "I ended up hiking the AT instead."

Callie bit her lip pensively and studied him. "Linden, are you ever going to ask me about Henry's father?"

Linden looked up in surprise and smiled, but it wasn't his usual smile and there was sadness in his eyes. "That's up to you," he said gently.

Tears filled Callie's eyes as she rewrapped her grinder. She suddenly wasn't hungry anymore. Through a blur of tears she looked at the blueness of the sky and didn't know what to say. Finally, haltingly, she began to relate the circumstances that had led to her indiscretion. Linden leaned back and listened. When she finished, she looked up, searching his eyes. "It was the worst mistake of my life, Linden. I am so sorry." Linden just closed his eyes. Even though he'd already heard Katie's version of what happened, it sounded different coming from Callie, and his heart ached at the thought of her being with someone else. He tried to push the image away, but it kept slipping back into his mind. "I ruined everything," she said quietly. "What I did is beyond forgiveness."

Linden crossed his arms over his chest and fought back tears of his own. He couldn't bring himself to look at Callie, so he looked at Henry. "If you didn't make that mistake," he said softly, "you wouldn't have Henry, and *he* is *not* a mistake. I just wish you'd told me. I wish you'd given me the chance . . ." His voice trailed off, but he knew in his heart that he would've forgiven her, even then. He stood up and looked across the valley.

"I'm sorry I didn't tell you, Linden." Callie paused, searching for the words. "I was afraid of what you'd say. I was afraid of the look in your eyes, so I hid the truth and ran away from everyone I love. I didn't think. I just didn't think." A new crop of tears streamed down her cheeks as she stared at Linden's back, aching for him say it was okay . . . aching for him to take her in his arms and say it didn't matter.

When Linden finally spoke, his voice was barely audible. "I never stopped loving you, Callie," he said softly, turning to look at her with tears in his eyes.

"I'm so sorry," she whispered, standing up. Linden closed his eyes and felt her gently brush his tears away. He pulled her body into his and breathed in her lovely scent. They stood there for a long time, their bodies slowly remembering the tender intimacy they'd once known.

Finally, Henry stirred and Linden stepped back. There was no more to say, and they were both quiet as Callie lifted Henry out and set him on the rocks. Henry blinked at the bright sunshine and Callie waited, bracing for a meltdown, but Springer wiggled over to greet him and Henry just rested his hand on the dog's soft head and looked out at the mountains. Callie let out a slow sigh of relief. "Are you hungry, Hen-Ben?" Henry climbed down to where she was standing and waited while she unwrapped the grinder again. "Why don't you sit there?" she suggested, motioning to the smooth, flat rock she'd been sitting on. Henry sat down and Callie handed him the sandwich while Springer, wagging his tail, found a spot nearby.

Linden sighed and shook his head. "That sandwich is for *you,* Henry, not Springer." Henry swung his legs, took a bite, and nodded, but when he was almost finished, he gave the last morsel to the big yellow Lab whose thumping tail gave away their furtive exchange. Linden eyed him suspiciously, but Springer just licked his lips and looked away innocently.

Linden stood up and motioned for Henry to follow him, and Callie watched and thought of the photo that was tucked into the frame of her mirror. *He looks just the same,* she thought. Henry squatted down next to Linden. "This is called a benchmark," Linden explained, pointing to a metal pin that had been tapped into the rock. "It tells the mountain's elevation—how high it is above the ocean." Henry ran his finger over the worn marker, and Linden continued. "Most big mountains have 'em. They're also known as U.S. geological survey markers. This one is so worn it's hard to read, but Monadnock is three thousand one hundred sixty-five feet above the ocean." Henry furrowed his brow and looked around for the ocean. "The ocean doesn't have to be nearby, Henry. It's just a measurement." He smiled, and Henry nodded. Linden stood up and glanced at his watch, and Henry looked at his bare wrist. "I guess we should get going," he said. Callie nodded and slipped the backpack onto her shoulders. Henry had begun to trot up and down on the rocks but, when a group of teenagers emerged from the woods, he stood shyly behind Linden. The two dogs, on the other hand, bounded over to greet them.

"Great dogs," one boy said. The others all nodded in agreement.

"Thanks," Linden replied. Henry slipped his hand into Linden's, and they rejoined Callie and started to hike down with the dogs leading the way. "Oh, to be a kid again," Linden murmured wistfully.

"Mmmm," Callie agreed. "Life was certainly much simpler."

• • •

"So, how about leftover spaghetti tonight?" Callie asked as they turned onto the dirt road that led to the cabin.

"If Reba's still holdin' her own . . . pardon the pun!"

Callie rolled her eyes, and Linden grinned. "Hey, can you do that again?" he teased. Callie shook her head and laughed. It felt good to laugh . . . and it almost felt like old times.

They pulled up to the cabin with the dogs hanging out the windows. When Linden released his seat belt, he realized that his shoulder was covered with slobber. "Thanks, buddy!" he said, pulling the seat forward so Springer could hop out. Callie let Kat out on the other side, but Henry, after hiking all the way down the mountain, had fallen asleep again.

"I hope he sleeps tonight, too," she said as she came around to the back of the car to unlock the trunk. Linden lifted out the child carrier and noticed the faded concert sticker on the back bumper.

"*That* was a fun concert," he said, nodding at the sticker.

"It was," Callie agreed with a sparkle in her eyes.

"I still can't believe we didn't get caught."

"Mmmm," Callie murmured, remembering their clandestine trip to Boston the summer she turned

189

eighteen. She searched Linden's eyes, and he wrapped her in his arms.

"I'm so glad you're home," he whispered.

"Me too," she said, feeling the aching burden of sorrow and shame lift from her shoulders, leaving her with the sensation that she could, once again, breathe.

Callie closed her eyes, and Linden kissed her softly on her eyelashes and on her cheeks before barely touching her lips . . . barely believing.

36

Callie heard a light knock on the screen door and peered out to see Linden standing in the driveway with his hands behind his back and a bottle of wine tucked under his arm. His chestnut brown hair was still damp from showering, and he was wearing a heather-gray T-shirt with the words *Go Pre* printed in faded green letters across the chest.

"Hey," he said with a smile.

"Hey," Callie replied, pushing open the door. "You didn't need to bring anything."

"I know," he said. "But I thought it would be nice to have a little red wine with dinner." He stepped inside. "You should take it though."

Callie slipped the bottle from under his arm and looked at the label. "Hmmm, a nice *French* cabernet to have with our *Italian* dinner," she teased.

Linden grinned. "Hey! At least it's not Boone's Farm."

Callie looked wistful. "Boone's Farm would've been fun—a little Country Kwencher to toast fond memories."

Linden shook his head and smiled. "And these are for you," he said, pulling a large bouquet of orange lilies from behind his back.

"Thank you! They're beautiful."

"*And*"—he paused dramatically—"a little dessert," he added, holding out a pint of Cherry Garcia.

"I knew I liked you for a reason," she said.

"Okay if I put it in the freezer?" Callie nodded, and he pulled open the freezer door. "Gee, I don't know if there's room," he teased. "Maybe next to this empty ice cube tray."

Callie laughed. "I haven't really had a chance to stock up yet," she said as she filled a vase with water.

"Well, next time I come I'm going to bring you some staples: frozen pizza, French fries, Eggo waffles, all the good stuff."

Callie looked up from fresh-cutting the stems. "Is that what you live on?"

"Sometimes I go all out and make scrambled eggs too," he said with a grin. "Where's Henry?"

"In the living room. I found a pad of paper when we got home, and he's been drawing ever since."

Linden went in to see Henry's drawing while

Callie finished heating up the spaghetti and tossing a salad. She warmed up some rolls and opened the wine. "Supper's ready!" she called. "Do you want to eat out on the porch?" Henry appeared and walked right over to the door. "I guess so!" she said with a smile. They carried everything outside and set it on the table. "Henry, can you give everyone a napkin?" she asked, handing him three napkins, and Henry walked dutifully around the table while Linden poured the wine and Callie lit the candles.

Over dinner, they talked about simpler times, and Linden filled Callie in on all the triumphs and failures of their high school classmates, including the news that Jon Connor was getting married.

"No way!" Callie exclaimed. She loved hearing about everyone, and more than once she commented, "Gosh, I haven't seen him in ages!"

To which Linden replied, "That's what happens when you don't come home for a visit."

"This was really nice," Callie said, finally, leaning back in her chair.

Linden nodded and refilled their glasses. "It *is* really nice."

Callie took a sip and sighed. "Well, as nice as it *is,* I really should help Henry get ready for bed." As if on cue, Henry slipped from his chair and pulled open the door and held it for her. Callie gave Linden a surprised look. "Thanks, buddy," she said, standing to clear as many things as she could carry before ushering him down the hall for a quick bath. "Just leave everything," she called over her shoulder.

Ten minutes later, Henry shuffled back to the kitchen in his pajamas and shyly eyed the three bowls of ice cream that were waiting on the counter. Callie hung up the bath towel and followed him. She looked around the kitchen and saw that all the dishes had been washed, and she shook her head. "You weren't supposed to do that!"

Linden just grinned and handed her a bowl.

After Henry was tucked in, Callie came back to the kitchen. "I don't think this house ever cools off," she said. "Do you want to sit outside?"

"I wish I could, but I should get going and make sure everything's okay back at the ranch."

Callie nodded. "Well, I really enjoyed today, and I know Henry did too."

Linden pulled her into a hug. "I did too," he murmured, leaning back against the counter and holding her close.

37

It was early afternoon before Callie finally parked under the sprawling limbs of the old oaks in Linden's yard. The summer air was oppressive, and Callie's sun-streaked hair had, once again, taken on a life of its own. She had tried to tame it by pulling it into a ponytail, but it was stubbornly resisting restraint. "What did I do to deserve this?" she asked, looking in the rearview mirror.

"Hey," Linden said with a smile, appearing next to the car.

"Hey!" she said, looking up in surprise. "What's the matter?"

"Nothing, just one of those days." Linden opened the passenger door, pulled the seat forward, and unhooked Henry's belt. He clambered out but wasn't on the ground for more than two seconds before the dogs bowled him over happily. He took their enthusiastic greeting in stride, but his short stature made his head especially vulnerable and he had to put his arms over his face to deflect the assault of their happy tails.

"How's Reba?" Callie asked, helping Henry up while Linden pulled the dogs back.

"She's hangin' in, although she's been telling us about it all morning." As if to prove his words true, a loud bellowing came from the barn. "Cindy said she'd be here this afternoon, and I hope it's soon." Linden's usually easygoing countenance was shadowed with worry.

"Are you sure it's okay to leave Henry? It sounds like you have your hands full."

"I'm sure," he replied. "Besides, maybe he'll get to watch a calf being born."

Callie looked skeptical.

"Don't worry," Linden reassured her. "We'll be fine."

She pressed her lips together, unconvinced. "Okay, well, he's had lunch, so he should be set for a while, and I made cookies for you." She leaned over the driver's seat, reaching for the plate. As she did her shirt pulled out, and Linden noticed the smooth, brown skin of her lower back. When she straightened up and handed the plate to him, he had a funny look on his face. Self-consciously, she touched her hair. "What?" she asked in dismay.

"Nothing," he answered, smiling. "We *love* cookies, don't we, guys?" The dogs wagged their tails and tried to nonchalantly lick the bottom of the plate, hoping to absorb some flavor.

Callie smiled. "I don't know how I'm ever going to make this up to you."

"Oh, well, I can probably come up with something."

Callie laughed. "Well, let me know when you do."

"Don't worry, I will," he said with a mischievous grin.

Callie rolled her eyes and smiled. "I won't be long," she said, pulling the seat back. "I'm just going to see my dad and then maybe run a couple of quick errands."

"Take your time."

She gave Henry a hug. "Be good!" She turned back to Linden. "Could you do something about this heat before I get back?"

"I'll try," he said with a wry smile.

Callie waved as she pulled away, and Linden waved back and watched her go. Then he turned to Henry. "C'mon, pal, let's go put these in the kitchen." Henry trailed along behind Linden and trudged up the porch steps with the dogs beside him. Linden held the screen door open, and the small parade trooped inside. Linden offered Henry a cookie before putting the plate on the counter. "Want some milk?" Henry took a bite and nodded and, while Linden was busy pouring, he gave a piece of his cookie to Kat and Springer. "That cookie's for you," Linden said, eyeing him. Henry nodded and placed his hand gently on Springer's head. Linden put two more cookies in a zip-and-seal bag, turned around, and realized he should have put the headset away, because Henry had already found it. "Hold on there, mister," Linden began. "Your mom doesn't . . ." but he didn't get to finish his sentence because a loud pickup truck was rumbling into the yard and the dogs had charged over to the door, tails wagging.

Cindy climbed out of her truck just as Linden pushed open the front door. The dogs bounded toward her and almost mowed her down. She laughed, looked up, and saw Linden coming across the yard with Henry in tow. She reached out to shake hands. "Hey, stranger!" she said with a smile as big as Texas. "Who's your little partner?"

Linden shook her hand and nodded to Henry. "This is Henry."

Cindy knelt down in front of Henry, but he backed shyly behind Linden's leg. "Hey, Henry," she said softly, offering her hand, but Henry had the headset and the bag with the two cookies in his hand and he'd put his other hand on Springer's head. Cindy stood up with a puzzled smile. "What's with the headset?"

Linden glanced down and shook his head. "Henry doesn't like loud noises."

Suddenly, a long mournful bellow filled the air, and Cindy looked in the direction of the barn. "That doesn't sound like a very happy camper. Have you got her inside?" she asked, striding away in the direction of the barn. Linden nodded, but Cindy wasn't looking at him so he said, "Yes," scooped Henry up, and hurried after her.

They found Reba lying down in her stall, breathing heavily. When they walked in, though, she kicked out her legs and struggled to stand. Her eyes were wild with fear and pain, and Cindy whistled softly. "You're ready, baby, aren't you?" She climbed into the stall, and Reba swayed precariously and bellowed loudly. "It's okay, baby, it's okay." She stroked Reba's swollen side and tried to see her hind end, but the stressed heifer backed uncooperatively into the corner, swinging her head heavily and gazing blindly past Cindy.

Linden was still holding Henry, but he tried to see her hind end through an adjacent stall. "She has a big white sac hanging out," he blurted in surprise.

Cindy nodded as she continued to move around the unhappy bovine. "Are there any hooves?"

Linden looked closer and shook his head. "It's hard to tell, but I don't think so." Suddenly, Reba lurched forward and fell to her knees, and Cindy quickly got behind her to see for herself.

"How long has she been like this?" she asked in an alarmed voice.

"I don't know. She's been bellowing all morning," Linden answered, startled by the sudden change in Cindy's tone. "But I checked on her, and that sac wasn't there."

"How long ago?"

Flustered, Linden stammered, "How . . . how long ago?"

"How long ago *did you check her?*"

"I don't know . . . maybe a half hour."

Cindy nodded and started to roll up her sleeves. "Linden, you are going to have to put that boy down and help me. In my truck are gloves, a bucket, and clean towels. And I need you to fill the bucket with hot water. *Now!*"

Linden set Henry down on a bale of hay and

lifted his chin to look him in the eye. "Stay there," he commanded. Henry's eyes grew wide, and he backed into the corner with his arms around his knees.

Linden sprinted to the truck and retrieved the items Cindy had asked for. Then he ran to the house and waited impatiently for the hot water to finally reach the tap. At last, with the bucket full of steaming water, he walked briskly across the yard. The air was heavy, and beads of perspiration trickled down the sides of his face. He heard a low, menacing rumble in the distance and looked across the meadow. Silent flashes of hot light illuminated a black, roiling mountain of clouds in the distance. Linden's heart pounded. *Not now!*

He hurried into the barn with the hot water sloshing onto his jeans and sneakers. Reba was still lying down, breathing heavily, and Cindy looked up. "The calf must be turned around." Her voice was tense. "I've only had this happen one other time." Linden nodded and glanced over at Henry, who had slipped the headset over his ears and was looking up at the rafters. Cindy reached for the bucket and gloves. Suddenly, a deafening thunderclap split the heavens above the barn, and Reba rose like a tidal wave and knocked Cindy back into the wall, spilling the water. The lights in the barn flickered. Cindy scrambled to her feet, pulled on the gloves, and plunged them into what was left of the hot water. She wrung out one of the towels and commanded, "Get in here and try to hold her steady." Linden climbed into the stall as Cindy stepped behind the weary heifer. With the warm, clean towel she wiped all around the sac and then proceeded to gently reach a gloved arm inside, looking for the calf's hooves.

38

Henry didn't like the sounds Reba was making, and he didn't like her stomping her feet. He glanced toward her stall and then quickly looked away, Linden's words echoing in his head. *Stay there!* He closed his eyes and began rocking back and forth. *Stay there! Stay there! Stay there!* Electricity snapped through the air, and a loud clap of thunder shook the barn to its foundation. Startled, Henry opened his eyes and, with his small hands, pressed the headset tighter against his head. He peeked at Reba and looked away. *Stay there! Stay there! Stay there!* He looked up into the rafters and, for the first time, noticed the geometric pattern they made. With his eyes, he began to trace each rafter and study each angle. The pattern soothed him, and he continued to follow it with his eyes, up, down, over, up, down, over, but then he noticed something out of place . . . there was something that didn't fit in the pattern. Henry stared into the shadows, trying to make out the object on the uppermost rafter. It looked like a piece of wood but then . . . it turned . . . and two eyes looked down and blinked at him. Henry could hear Linden's voice. *Who cooks for you?* Suddenly, the owl stretched its broad wings, pushed off the rafter, and flew silently out through the open hay door, into the rain. Henry slipped off the hay bale and stood in the doorway, watching Atticus sweep across the meadow and land in the top of the tall Norway spruce. Henry blinked and softly whispered the words out loud, "Who cooks for you? Who cooks for you all?"

39

As Callie hurried across the hospital parking lot she felt sprinkles falling on her skin and smelled the warm, steamy scent of cool rain splashing on hot pavement. She looked up at the dark clouds encroaching on the summer blue sky and thought of the Thomas Cole painting that hung in the hospital waiting room.

As she approached the entrance, the doors opened and a gray-haired woman slowly pushed an older gentleman in a wheelchair through the doors. Callie waited politely, silently scolding herself for feeling impatient. The couple smiled warmly and thanked her as they passed, and Callie nodded before bolting down the hall to the elevator. She pushed the button and waited, watching the light click slowly down and wondering if she should have taken the stairs. At last, the door opened, but Callie had to step aside to let a nurse who was struggling to maneuver a cumbersome food cart make her way out. Once inside the elevator, Callie pushed the button for the third floor but, just as the door was about to close, a man and young boy ran up and she had to reach out to hold the door open. The man thanked her, pushed the button for the second floor, and rested his hands on the boy's shoulders. Callie could feel the boy's eyes studying her as the elevator climbed. He was probably wondering why she was there, just as she was wondering why they were there. *Are they visiting the boy's mom?* She shook her head sadly. *Why do people have to deal with illness and tragedy? Why can't they just be well their whole lives and, when it's their time to go, simply leave the world peacefully while sleeping? That's what I would've done,* she thought. "That's how I would've handled old age," she said out loud without realizing it, but then noticing that the boy gave the man a funny look. The door opened and the man smiled as he ushered the boy out, and a nurse bustled in and pushed the 3 again, even though it was already lit. Callie, who had been staring at the floor, looked up and realized it was Jess.

"Hey, Jess!" she said with a smile.

The nurse turned around. "Hey, baby!" She wrapped Callie in a hug. "Your daddy's doin' so good! Have you seen him?"

"I'm going now."

Jess nodded and then looked puzzled. "Do you know they moved him out of ICU?"

"No, I just got here."

"Well, he's not on three anymore either. He's back down on two."

"Oh," Callie said with a sigh. "I didn't know. If I did, I would've brought Henry."

"That's all right, baby. You can bring that honey with you later. Just go see your dad and tell him you'll bring his handsome grandson with you next time. That'll make him happy." The door opened, and Jess gave Callie another hug.

Callie pushed the button for the second floor and leaned against the wall. While she waited for the elevator to go down, she noticed an outdated poster for the hospital's Fourth of July picnic hanging on the opposite wall. She had loved going to the hospital picnics when she was little. They'd played volleyball, gone swimming, pedaled paddleboats, eaten lots of food, and one year she'd even beaten her dad at horseshoes.

The elevator door opened and her memory of the picnics slipped away as quickly as it had come. She hurried down the hall, peering into rooms, and finally found her dad in the very last one. He was in a bed near the window and he was watching the news with the volume turned low so he wouldn't disturb his neighbor.

"Hey, Dad!" she said softly, giving him a hug.

"Hey, kiddo!" he said with a big smile.

They continued to talk in hushed voices. "You look really good."

"I feel good too." He looked around. "I'm out of intensive care, you know."

Callie nodded. "I know, but I didn't know before I came. I'll bring him next time."

"Did you go hiking?"

"Yup."

"And how'd it go?"

"It was fun. Linden had a child carrier, and although Henry hiked for a while, he finally decided to get in and take a ride, and then he fell asleep." She paused thoughtfully. "Linden and I finally had a chance to talk too, but it wasn't easy." Ben nodded, and Callie smiled. "I think he might've forgiven me."

"I knew he would."

"And Henry is so good with him. I just can't get over how they are together." She looked out the window. "There's a storm comin' in."

"I know. The weatherman's been talking about it all day."

"I used to love thunderstorms. Do you remember how we used to sit on the porch and watch them come over the hill?"

"I remember," he said with a smile.

204

"Do you remember how the hummingbirds used to come to the feeder, even in the middle of a storm? They didn't mind getting wet. I think they enjoyed it. They just spread out their wings as if they were taking a shower."

Ben laughed. "Do you remember the one that hovered right next to your head?"

Callie nodded. "I think he liked my red ribbon. He sounded just like a big bumblebee."

Ben paused thoughtfully. "Your mom didn't like thunderstorms though."

"I know. She always wanted us to come in. Now that I'm a mom, I can understand why."

Ben searched his daughter's eyes. "You're a good mom too, Callie. Don't ever think you're not."

"I don't know, Dad. I'm not very patient, I lose my temper easily, and half the time I can't figure out what's bothering him. It sure would be easier if he would just start talking."

Ben nodded thoughtfully. "Well, don't forget to seek out Maddie Coleman. I know she'll be able to give you some ideas."

"I will." Callie nodded. "But right now I just want to know what the doctor has to say about *you.*"

Ben held up his hands. "Rehab, I think."

"Same place?"

"I guess," Ben answered with a shrug.

"How soon?"

"I'm not sure, but don't worry about me." He

smiled, and Callie noticed the color in his cheeks. "You just take care of my grandson."

Callie laughed. "Okay, Dad, but we're going to get you well enough to come home too." She sat down on the edge of his bed and took his hand. "Do you remember when I used to hold your hand in church?"

"How could I not? You could hardly sit still."

Callie ran her finger over his knuckles. "I used to pretend these were the mountains in the Presidential Range."

Ben laughed. "I know. You couldn't keep quiet either."

"I was bored."

"Are you still?"

She smiled and shook her head. "I don't get to church much anymore, with Henry."

"You weren't easy, you know, and we still took you."

Callie looked down. "This is different, Dad."

Ben searched her eyes. "It's important, Cal. No matter what trials you're facing, God gives you the strength to get through them, and a church family is always there to help. I honestly don't know if I'd have made it through your mom's passing without the love and support of our friends at church." Callie nodded, remembering the endless supply of casseroles and pies, the long snowy walks her dad had taken with friends, and the countless phone calls to "just check in."

"Okay, Dad. We'll try."

"Good!" Ben looked pleased.

They talked for a while more until Ben finally said, "You should get going, Cal. You've wasted enough time hangin' around here."

"I'm not wasting time," Callie replied. "But I am going to go. One of Linden's cows is getting ready to calve, and I'm a little worried about Henry's reaction."

Ben nodded. "Maybe when you get home, you can find that hummingbird feeder. I bet Henry would get a kick out of it."

"I will." She leaned over and gave her dad a hug. "Love you, Dad."

"Love you too, kiddo!" he said softly.

40

Linden held on to Reba as best he could while Cindy worked at her other end.

"I have both hooves," she shouted over the sound of the rain pounding on the roof. Linden nodded as she started to pull. After several minutes, she shouted in frustration, "It won't budge and we've got to get it out of there."

"Want me to try?" Linden shouted back.

But Cindy didn't seem to hear him. Instead of answering, she looked around and asked, "Do you have any baling twine?"

Linden nodded and climbed out of the stall to

cut twine off of a hay bale. He reached for the scissors hanging on the wall, and his heart suddenly stopped. *Where is Henry?* He looked around the barn. "Henry!" he called, but there was no response.

"Linden! The twine!" Linden cut the twine, yanked it off the hay bale, and hopped back over the railing. With shaking hands, he stood beside Cindy, trying to remember his Boy Scout knots. "Just tie it!" she shouted, but his mind and heart were racing. He glanced at the hay bale again, hoping to see Henry sitting there, but the spot was still empty. Fumblingly, he finally tied two half hitches around each hoof and they both began to pull. Linden could feel the twine tightening around his hands, and he could also feel the calf beginning to move.

"Keep pulling! It's coming!" Cindy shouted. Linden glanced over at Cindy's hands and realized she had gloves on. He felt the twine cutting into his hands and wished he'd thought to do the same. Reba looked back and widened her stance while Linden and Cindy continued to pull. Before long, the calf's hind legs were out and Linden tried to pull on its haunches, but it was too slippery and he ended up having to pull on the twine again. Finally, when it was almost halfway out, they both realized that *it* was a *he,* and the rest of him slid out like a big glob of milky Jell-O and landed on the clean shavings in a wet heap. Reba immediately turned around and began licking away the sac and Cindy made sure he was breathing.

"I'm going to look for Henry!" Linden shouted.

Cindy caught sight of Linden's hands, and he followed her gaze. His palms were striped with angry cuts, and his tan knuckles were smeared with blood. He shook his head, turned, and climbed numbly out of the stall. He didn't feel any pain. The only sensations he felt were nausea and fear. Cindy left the new calf in his mother's care and, together, they searched every corner of the barn, calling his name over and over . . . but there was no sign of him.

Linden shook his head in disbelief. "Callie warned me that he wanders off. Damn! I should've been watching him. I'm going down to the river and then I'll check the house."

Cindy followed him into the rain. "I'll look in the woods and the meadow." Linden nodded and they parted, each frantically calling. Linden sprinted to the river, his heart pounding. An image of Henry's lifeless body floating in the water flashed through his mind and he felt another wave of nausea. He stumbled down the riverbank, calling and searching for any sign of him. He ran downstream, ripping through the brush and scanning the river's width and depth for anything that looked out of place, praying that Henry hadn't been drawn to the river. Finally, he headed back along the footpath, still calling. He saw Cindy, and she just shook her head. He leapt up the porch stairs and looked in every room and closet, but the house was achingly silent. *Henry, where are you?*

Cindy came up on the porch. "Linden," she said in dismay, "I hate to say this, but you better call 911."

41

The storm had passed when Callie emerged from the hospital and she wondered if the worst of it had missed them. She walked quickly to her car, making a list in her head of the things she needed, glanced at her watch, and realized it was already after six. *How did it get so late?*

She hurried through the store, picked up a few items, and then stopped for gas. While it was pumping, she rolled down her car windows. As promised, the storm had ushered in cooler air, and it swept breezily through the windows, blowing her hair around her face as she drove. She turned on the radio and an old Journey song drifted out. She smiled wistfully and sang along, remembering her own long-ago, carefree, summer nights.

She glanced in her rearview mirror and suddenly realized that the cars behind her were pulling over. She looked up at the sky to see if there was another rainbow, but the sky was dark. She turned off the radio and, within seconds, the eerie wail of sirens filled the silence. She pulled over to the side of the road and watched as two police cars and an ambulance sped by. She whispered a prayer, as she always did, for whoever needed help, and then continued on.

She forgot all about the radio and drove in silence, the sirens still echoing in her head. For some reason she couldn't seem to shake the foreboding that had settled on her heart . . . and, when she pulled onto the dirt road, the feeling overwhelmed her. There were emergency vehicles parked on both sides of the road, and their lights were flashing across the sky and through the trees. Callie began to shake. *Oh, no! What happened?* There was no room to get past all of the vehicles in the driveway, so she finally just abandoned her car with the engine still running and ran the rest of the way. Linden was standing near a trailer, talking to several policemen, but when he saw her he broke away. "Oh, Callie, I'm sorry. I'm so sorry." He was soaking wet, and his eyes were wild with panic and disbelief. "Reba was in trouble and I looked away for a second, and then he was gone!"

Through a blur of tears, Callie read the words on the side of the trailer and tried to comprehend their meaning: EMERGENCY RESCUE DIVE TEAM. *Oh, no! The river! This cannot be happening . . . it's just a bad dream . . . please let me wake up and find out it's not true.* She felt her knees give way, and then she felt strong arms circling around her and holding her up. Linden and one of the officers guided her to the back of the ambulance. "Miss, are you the boy's mother?" a familiar voice asked. She looked up at the officer and tried to place his face. It was drawn and weary, and he was older. *Where do I know him from?* She nodded, and he took a notebook and pen from his pocket. "I'm very sorry, but I need to ask you some questions."

Callie started to shake uncontrollably, and someone wrapped a blanket around her shoulders. Then the officer began to ask her the same questions he had just asked Linden: *What is the boy's name and age? What was he wearing? Did he take any medications? Please explain the condition he has. Can he hear? Has he ever run away before?* Callie hugged her chest and numbly answered, and then she looked around and cried out, "Why aren't you looking for him?" She threw the blanket off and stumbled toward the river, but Linden reached out and pulled her into his arms. "They *are* looking for him, Callie. There are lots of people scouring the woods, and there are search dogs too. We're going to find him, Callie. I don't know if this is any consolation, but he's not alone. Springer is missing too."

An officer walked briskly toward them. "The news is here. Would either of you be able to make a statement?" Linden nodded gravely, but Callie just covered her face and turned away.

42

Ben looked at the clock and decided it was time for bed. He needed to use the john one last time though. He pushed the call button but the nurse didn't come, so he decided he'd try to make it on his own. He sat up, slowly swung his legs over the side, reached for his walker, and stood up gingerly. *Not bad!* He glanced at his neighbor, Hal, who appeared to be dozing, but then Hal opened one eye and peered at him. "Ben, you're such a rebel," he teased.

"Well, the nurses don't come and a fella can't wait forever."

"I know what you mean."

Ben made his way slowly across the room and disappeared into the bathroom.

Hal chuckled and raised his bed up a bit. "Mind if I turn on the news?" he called.

"No, go ahead," Ben said, closing the door. Hal clicked on the TV and watched as *Breaking News* scrolled across the bottom of the screen. A field reporter, standing in front of the New Hampshire State Police emergency dive trailer, spoke to the camera. "Three-year-old Henry Wyeth was last seen this afternoon during the storm. He has blond hair and blue eyes, and he was wearing a John Deere T-shirt, green shorts, and blue sneakers. He is said to have autism and he doesn't speak. The dive team is here as a precaution because the Contoocook River runs through the property, and although there are still people out looking with flashlights tonight, a full-scale search will be launched early tomorrow morning. Volunteers are asked to arrive by seven o'clock, but if anyone has any information about the boy or thinks they've seen him, please call the Jaffrey Police."

Hal heard the toilet flush and the water running, and then Ben reemerged with a smile. "See, even an old coot can still take care of himself!"

Hal laughed. "You mean a *stubborn* old coot."

Just then the nurse came in and, when she saw him out of bed, hurried over to help him. "Mr. Wyeth, you shouldn't be out of bed without assistance," she scolded him. Ben just nodded obediently and winked at Hal.

43

It was well after dark when the search was finally called off. Linden helped Callie into the house, and she collapsed on the couch across from Cindy. Linden covered them both with blankets and then sat on the couch too. He raked his hands through his hair, feeling helpless. A moment later, Kat pulled herself up and walked over to sit between them. She rested her head on Callie's lap as fresh tears rolled down Callie's cheeks. Callie reached out to stroke the noble head in her lap, and Kat stayed there all night.

It was dark under the trees, but out in the clearing the sky was filled with stars and the moon shone brightly. Henry couldn't hear the voices anymore, and he couldn't hear the owls either. The only sound he heard was the wind in the trees. He pointed to the moon and whispered, "Good night, moon." He lay down on the grass and looked at the patterns the stars made. His eyes moved from one to another, his mind following the invisible angles until his eyelids grew heavy and fluttered closed. Springer rested his chin on Henry's chest and never moved.

44

The telephone rang before dawn, startling Linden into consciousness. He sat up, looked around, and felt his stomach twist into knots as the events of the day before hit him. The phone rang impatiently, and he got up to answer it before it woke Callie. The early-morning light illuminated the kitchen as he listened to an officer on the other end of the line say they would be out within the hour to resume the search. Linden nodded and hung up. Then he gazed through the window at the sunrise reflecting on the misty river and whispered, "Oh, Henry, where are you?"

Finally, he turned determinedly from the window and pulled down the attic stairs, hoping they wouldn't squeak. He'd seen a party-size perk pot when he dug out the child carrier, and he knew that coffee would be welcomed by the early volunteers. He carried the cumbersome pot down the stairs, rinsed off the cobwebs and dust, filled it with cold water, opened a new bag of coffee, guessed at the measurement, and plugged the pot in on the porch. While it sputtered to life, he carried out sugar, milk, spoons, cups, and napkins.

The volunteers began arriving well before seven, and they were immediately given bright orange vests and instructions on staying safe. They were also told that there was a good chance Henry was with a big yellow Labrador retriever named Springer and they should try calling the dog's name because he could very well lead them to Henry. Linden stood by, listening and desperately wanting to join the search, but not wanting to leave Callie alone. Cindy came up beside him, wearing a vest. "I'm going to look," she said. Linden nodded. "Thanks, Cindy."

Callie stood near the ambulance, holding a cup of the hot coffee and answering the same questions all over again. Finally, the officer left her alone and she sat down on the bumper. With trembling hands she sipped her coffee and watched Reba nursing her new calf in the early morning sun.

45

Henry opened his eyes and looked up at the azure-blue sky. The rain was gone and the darkness was gone but he was not gone and Springer was not gone. He sat up and noticed the bag of cookies on the ground. He pulled the bag open and Springer perked up, his tail slowly thumping. Henry reached into the bag with his small hand and took out several broken pieces and gave them to Springer, and then he ate one and gave Springer the rest. He looked around and saw several smooth stones lying near his feet and reached down to touch one. He picked it up and held it right in front of his eyes. Then he put it down again. He picked up another one, studied it, and placed it on top of the first one. He continued to reach for stones until all the stones within reach were in a small pile. He got up then and walked around, gathering more stones and making the pile bigger. Springer lay with his big head on his paws and followed Henry's every move with his eyes. Finally, Henry added one last stone to the top of the pile and wandered off to start a new pile. The big yellow Lab pulled himself up and followed.

46

"Callie?" a voice called from the driveway.

Callie looked up from the cup in her hands and saw Dr. Franklin, wearing jeans and a pressed oxford shirt, walking toward her. She stood up quickly, spilling the cold coffee on her sneakers. She looked down but seemed too lost to care. Out of habit, she reached up to smooth her hair and then tried to muster a weak smile. "Dr. Franklin," she said in surprise. "What are you doing here?"

"I came as soon as I could," he said, giving Callie a hug.

"You didn't have to," she said.

"I heard about Henry on the news and I called the hospital right away to check on your dad. The nurses said he wasn't aware, and I hope you don't mind, but I asked them to try to keep it that way. Such news can be devas . . ."

Just then, two boys came running out of the woods, racing each other through the meadow. "They found him!" they shouted. "They found Henry!"

Callie heard their shouts and didn't know whether to laugh or cry. She ran toward the boys with tears spilling down her cheeks. Voices began to echo in all directions as the news spread. "They found him! They found Henry!" Callie's heart leapt at the music of the sound. Moments later, the search and rescue dogs bounded playfully out of the woods with Springer in the mix, and a crowd gathered around Callie, everyone wanting to witness the happy reunion. Finally, a group of smiling, orange-vested volunteers came out of the woods, and an older gentleman wearing a dark blue Jaffrey Volunteer Fire Department T-shirt and red suspenders emerged carrying Henry. Callie brushed away her tears and walked toward them with her heart bursting. The fireman lifted Henry into her arms and she held him close, breathing in his wonderful, warm little boy scent. She opened her eyes and looked at his sweet face, and hugged him tightly. "Oh, Henry, I love you so much," she whispered.

She looked around at all of the volunteers, and then with Henry hitched up on her hip—because she wasn't letting go of him anytime soon—she went around and hugged every single one. At last, she came to Linden, who had been standing apart from the others, and she hugged him the longest. Then she knelt down in front of Springer, looked in his deep brown eyes, and whispered, "Springer, you are a hero!"

Henry laid his hand on Springer's head and whispered, "Springer, Hero." Callie could hardly believe her ears, and when she looked up at Linden, he just smiled.

An EMT gently touched Callie's shoulder, and Callie turned to look at her. "Henry looks fine,

Miss Wyeth, but we need to take him to the hospital to be checked out. It's procedure."

Callie nodded, and Dr. Franklin came up beside her. "I'll follow you, and then you can take Henry to see your dad." Callie agreed and climbed into the back of the ambulance with Henry.

47

"Well, look who finally came to see his papa," Ben said when Henry appeared shyly in his doorway. "I heard you've been causing some excitement."

Henry reached for Callie's hand, and she nodded as they walked across the room. Henry ran his other hand lightly over the soft blanket, and Callie lifted him onto the bed. "Guess what?" Ben looked up questioningly, and Callie grinned. "When I was thanking everyone who helped look for him, I knelt down in front of Springer and told him he was a hero . . . and Henry repeated it!"

Ben looked at Henry. "You did?" Henry nodded slightly, and Ben beamed. "That's wonderful! Just think, someday when he's giving you back talk, you'll have to remember how glad you are now!"

Callie laughed and then nodded at the empty bed. "Where's your neighbor?"

Ben smiled. "He went home."

Just then Dr. Franklin knocked on the door. "Am I interrupting?"

"Not at all," Ben said.

"I'm not here officially," he said, pulling his stethoscope from around his neck and putting it in his ears, "but I thought I should check your blood pressure after so much excitement." Ben held out his arm, and Dr. Franklin slid on the cuff. He listened, watching the gauge intently, and then slipped the cuff off again. "It's a little high," he said, trying not to alarm them. "I'm just going to have the nurse give you something to get it down, and I'll check it again in a little while." He pulled the stethoscope back around his neck. "Sometimes after surgery it takes a bit of adjusting to get the right dose." He looked at Callie, his kind eyes seeming to read her thoughts. "Don't worry." She nodded, but this time his words didn't fill her with the same sense of peace.

"Maybe we should go and let you rest," she said quietly.

"That might be a good idea," the doctor said with a nod. "Besides, I also came to see if you'd like a ride home."

"You don't need to do that," she said. "I can call someone."

"There's no need. I go right by."

"All right," Callie said. "That would be a help." She looked at Henry. "Hen-Ben, can you give Papa a hug?" Henry leaned over and gave

221

his grandfather a gentle hug. Callie smiled and lifted him down and then hugged her dad too. "Love you, Dad."

"Love you too, honey."

48

"I want you to call me if you need anything," Dr. Franklin said, pulling a piece of paper from his shirt pocket with his home phone number on it. "Day or night," he added with a gentle smile.

Callie nodded. "I can't thank you enough."

He looked over at her. "Callie, you should know that your dad's heart is still very fragile and, although he probably feels better than he has in a long time, he needs to be very cautious and not rush things."

Callie nodded again. "Or *do* dumb things like getting out of bed without help."

"Exactly," the doctor said.

"He's stubborn, though."

Dr. Franklin smiled. "I know. That's another reason he reminds me of my own dad."

They pulled onto her road, and Callie saw her car already parked in the driveway. Beside it was Linden's truck. Dr. Franklin turned his old Subaru around in the driveway. "Looks like you have company."

She pressed her lips together and nodded. "Thank you again," she said, lifting Henry out and

222

waving as he pulled away. She watched him hesitate at the corner and was puzzled when he turned to head back the way they had come.

Linden was sitting on the steps, but when Callie came up the driveway with Henry asleep on her shoulder, he stood to meet her. "Callie, I'm so sorry all this happened."

Callie shook her head. "It's not your fault, Linden. It just happened. Out of the goodness of your heart, you were trying to help me."

"I should've been watching him."

Callie shook her head again. "You can't think that way. What if I blamed myself? I knew you had your hands full but I left him with you anyway. Maybe it's *my* fault."

Linden closed his eyes and shook his head in dismay. "It's definitely not your fault."

Callie stood in front of him and smiled. "He was found—that's all that matters." She paused. "But the whole time he was missing, I kept praying that if he was found . . . if I was given another chance to be his mom . . . I would do a better job. I would be more patient, I would learn all I could about autism, and, like *you* said, I would try to make a difference in other people's lives, maybe *little* people's lives."

She felt tears stinging her eyes. "The only thing is . . . I don't know if I can do all that and work on rebuilding our relationship too. I'm sorry, Linden. I guess what I'm trying to say is that I need time to figure this out. I need to be there for Henry—and my dad—before I can be there for anyone else." Linden pushed his hands into his pockets, and Callie couldn't help but see the sadness in his eyes. "You've done so much for me this last week. I can't believe it's only been one week. It feels like an eternity. But I hope you know how much I appreciate everything you've done."

49

When Linden pulled into the yard, the dogs moseyed over to him with their tails wagging. After all of the excitement that morning, they'd been a bit deflated when, one by one, all of their new friends left.

Cindy had been a huge help, cleaning up coffee cups and napkins and following Linden over to drop off Callie's car. On the ride back she told Linden how terrible she felt and asked him if he would like her to find a new home for the cows. He had looked at the little sun dappled calf standing beside his mother and shook his head.

Springer leaned against Linden's legs and he knelt down to stroke his soft ears and look into his sweet brown eyes. "You *are* a hero, you know that?" he whispered, and Springer licked his face and wagged his tail in agreement.

"Want to go for a walk?" he asked. The dogs circled around in happy anticipation and then fell into step beside him as he headed up the hill. The old fireman had described to Linden the area where he'd found Henry, and Linden wanted to see it for himself. He had described it as a grassy clearing, and said Linden would know it if he saw several small piles of stones.

"C'mon, Springer, show me!" he said, and Springer bounded ahead with his nose to the ground. Linden didn't really think the happy-go-lucky Lab knew what he was asking of him, but maybe Henry's familiar scent would lead Springer back to where they'd been found.

A half an hour later, they came to a clearing, and Linden saw something lying in the grass. He walked over and realized it was the light green pilot headset. He picked it up and smiled. *At least Callie won't have to fight this battle anymore.* He followed Springer along the perimeter of the clearing and soon found one of the piles of stones the fireman had talked about. It looked like a miniature cairn. Next to it was an empty plastic bag. Springer nosed around the bag, his tail wagging, and then swallowed something that Linden guessed was a piece of cookie. Linden saw another pile of stones a short distance away. He walked over to it and knelt down to fix some of the stones, and then he shook his head in wonder. *Had Henry been trying to mark his way?*

As the sun set, Linden and the dogs returned to the yard. Linden pulled a frosty beer from the river, leaned back in one of the Adirondack chairs, watched the dogs splashing in the clear water, and then gazed at the pile of stones he'd been working on before Callie had slipped back into his life. He took a long drink and whispered, "Guess it's just you and me, Ebenezer."

50

Callie carried Henry inside, laid him on the couch, and turned the fan on low. Then she opened the windows, poured a glass of cold lemonade, and sat at the table. She looked at the lilies; they were already drooping, and she wondered if Linden knew how daylilies had come by their name. She took a sip of her drink and its cool sweetness reminded her of what her dad had asked her to do. She got up to look in the cabinet where all the odds and ends were stored, and there, on the middle shelf, she saw the familiar red top of the hummingbird feeder. She pulled it out and turned to consult the faded recipe taped to the inside of the door. It was written in her mom's neat handwriting:

Hummer Nectar

1 cup water to ¼ cup sugar
Bring to a boil. Cool.
Change every three days or as needed.

Callie took out a small saucepan and a measuring cup, measured the sugar and water, and put both in the pot to boil. She rinsed off the feeder, put it in the dish drain to dry, and then stirred the mixture. After it came to a boil, she moved it off the burner and peeked in on Henry. He was still asleep. She latched the kitchen door, sank into her dad's favorite chair, and immediately fell asleep too.

The afternoon slipped quietly by, the sun streaked its last fiery rays across the horizon, and the world grew dark and still. An owl called, but Callie and Henry didn't hear it. Exhausted, they were both sound asleep. Finally, Callie began to dream that someone was knocking on the door . . . but, for some reason, she couldn't seem to move. The knocking continued and, with a start, she suddenly realized that someone *really* was knocking on the door. She opened her eyes and blinked, trying to adjust her eyes to the darkness and wondering how she had slept so long. She got up, glanced at the clock on the kitchen stove, and shook her head in disbelief. It was after ten. *Who would be here at this hour?* She heard a familiar voice calling her name, and when she switched on the porch light, she saw Dr. Franklin standing on the steps, his face drawn and tired, his blue eyes glistening with tears.

PART III

Two roads diverged in a wood, and I—
I took the one less traveled by,
And that has made all the difference.

—Robert Frost

51

Dr. Franklin stayed with Callie until he was sure she would be okay. It was almost morning when he finally stood in the doorway and gave her one last hug. "Please let me know if there's anything I can do and what arrangements you make. I know it's a difficult time, but I bet if you look through your dad's papers you'll find that he prepared for this. He would not have wanted you to have to figure it out all on your own."

After he left, Callie went through the motions of caring for Henry, but then she just went back to staring out the window. Finally, late in the day, she decided to make coffee. She had just clicked the button to brew and put the coffee can back in its spot when she heard a knock at the door. She peered through the screen and saw a tall man whose pants were an inch too short standing on the steps with two dishes in his hands. His white hair shone in the late-afternoon sun. "Hello, Callie," he said solemnly.

Although she had not seen him since her mom's funeral, Callie recognized the kind face immediately. She unlatched the door and held it open. "Hi, Reverend Taylor."

The old minister stepped inside. "I'm just coming by to offer my condolences and to check on you. I'm so sorry about your dad." He looked down at the plates in his hands. "Oh, and Sue sent these over, two of my favorites: fried chicken, macaroni and cheese, summer squash and"—he smiled as he held up the second dish—"blueberry pie."

"Thank you," she said, putting them on the counter.

"Well, my dear," he said with a gentle smile, "food is one of the things we Congregationalists do best."

"Would you like a cup of coffee?" Callie asked, trying to remember what her parents would do in this situation. "It's almost done brewing."

"No, no thank you," he said in a slow, measured voice. "I try to stay away from caffeine late in the day."

"Would you like some lemonade, then?" she asked, her own voice trailing off.

He shook his head, and Callie nodded and found herself fighting back tears again. "Your dad was a wonderful man and we all loved him very much. I just wanted you to know that I'm available to help with the arrangements or anything at all. I've been through this a few times."

Callie nodded and suddenly realized that these were things she'd have to take care of soon. "Can I come by your office tomorrow?"

"Well, church is in the morning," he said, trying to remember his schedule, "but I'm available after that. Say, after lunch?" Callie nodded, and he pushed open the door, but then looked back and smiled. "Make sure you eat. When word gets out, you won't know what to do with all the food."

Callie promised she would and then watched his car back out of the driveway. She looked at the clock and realized it was already six-thirty. Almost twenty-four hours had passed since her world had been turned upside down.

She looked at the plates and then noticed the pot of sugar water still on the stove. She poured it into the feeder, slipped the top on, and went out on the porch to hang it on its hook. Then she went back inside and looked in on Henry, who had fallen asleep on the couch again. She shook him gently. "Hen-Ben, wake up," she said. "It's time for supper." Henry rubbed his eyes and sat up. "Let's go use the bathroom," she said. Callie was surprised when he got right up and headed down the hall. When he was done, she lifted him onto the counter and washed his face and hands with a warm sudsy washcloth. When she was finished, he looked up at her, his tan face framed with damp blond hair, and smiled. Callie felt as if *she* had just been given the best gift in the world. She smiled back and hugged him. "Let's go have some supper."

Although she wasn't very hungry, the comfort food Sue had sent over was still warm . . . and delicious; Callie ended up eating more than she had in days. And Henry, for his part, had seconds of everything and still had room for blueberry pie.

While Callie did the dishes, Henry drew in the pad Callie had found for him. But as soon as she was finished, he wandered into the kitchen carrying *Goodnight Moon.* "Are you ready for a story?" she asked, drying her hands on the dish towel. Henry nodded and followed her outside to sit on the porch. Callie lifted him onto her lap, opened the book, and began to read. Henry was just getting ready to point to the mouse on the next page when an odd sound buzzed above their heads. Henry looked up with a frown and Callie whispered, "That's a hummingbird." The little hummer landed on the feeder, took a long drink, and then stopped to hover right in front of them as if trying to decide if they were friends or foes. Then, as quickly as it had come, it zipped away to see what the bee balm had to offer. Callie thought of her dad, smiled, and pulled Henry closer.

When they finished the book, Henry closed it and studied the picture on the cover of a room, a window, and the moon. Then he leaned back contentedly and listened to the buzzing and chirring sounds of the summer evening. Suddenly, far away, an owl called and Henry sat up and pointed in the direction of the sound.

Callie whispered, "What does an owl say?"

And Henry answered softly, "Who cooks for you? Who cooks for you *aaaalll?*"

52

The morning of the funeral dawned sunny and cool, and even though Callie arrived early, the sanctuary was already overflowing onto the lawn, and men were hurrying to set up chairs and speakers outside. It seemed that the whole town was turning out to pay their last respects to Benjamin Wyeth. Callie looked around and saw former and current students, former and current teachers, old veterans, young veterans, and dear friends dating back to Ben's college days. The obvious depth of love that was felt for her father overwhelmed her. She wished Henry could be there too, but she knew she'd made the right decision in leaving him with Maddie.

Callie and Henry had been sitting on the porch reading *Mike Mulligan and His Steam Shovel* after supper on Sunday when Maddie Coleman had pulled into the driveway. Henry had heard the car and squirmed off Callie's lap to see who was there, and then he'd run back to hide behind Callie's legs. "Hi, Mrs. Coleman," Callie had said with a smile while Henry peered around her.

"Oh, Callie, please call me Maddie. 'Mrs. Coleman' sounds so old!" She had given Callie a warm hug and then held her at arm's length. "I am so, so sorry about your dear dad. He was a wonderful man and a top-notch teacher, and we all loved him."

Callie had smiled, nodding appreciatively, and Maddie had turned to Henry. "And this handsome fellow must be Henry," she'd said softly, kneeling down in front of him. "I've heard so much about you!" Henry had shyly studied her friendly face and salt-and-pepper hair. "Can you give me five?" she asked, putting out her hand. To Callie's surprise, Henry had gently slapped her hand.

Maddie had stood, smiling. "He's beautiful, Callie. Your dad talked about him all the time. He thought the world of him." She paused. "I'm sorry to stop by unannounced, but Reverend Taylor mentioned in church today that you might be looking for someone to stay with Henry on Tuesday, and I wanted you to know that I would be honored to spend the day with Ben Wyeth's grandson."

Callie had looked surprised. "Don't you want to go to the funeral?"

Maddie had shaken her head and answered, "No, Callie. Staying with Henry would mean much more to me. I would feel as if I'm giving my own personal tribute to a man I loved very much."

Callie had nodded thoughtfully, not knowing whether to accept Maddie's gracious offer. She was certainly worried about Henry's reaction to a church full of people and music, but she'd already resigned herself to the idea that she didn't have any choice but to bring him.

"Henry isn't easy to look after. Although he's been using words a little bit," she said, "it's often hard to know what's bothering him."

Maddie had nodded and responded gently, "Callie, I know all about autism. That's part of the reason I came by—to meet Henry. But, more importantly, so he could meet me."

Maddie hadn't needed to say any more. Callie had immediately felt at peace with the decision, and later she couldn't help but wonder if her dad had played a part in bringing Maddie serendipitously into their lives.

The service was beautiful, and although Callie didn't get through it without some tears, she was definitely more in control of her emotions than she had been at her mom's funeral. Afterward, the receiving line seemed endless, and Callie's heart went out to everyone who had to wait in the hot sun, but when the line finally wound down, she looked up and realized that the person who had waited the longest was Linden. She gave him a hug. "Thank you for coming. I'm sorry you had to wait."

"That's okay," he said with a half smile. "I'm used to waiting."

53

When Callie finally got home after the long day, she found Maddie and Henry on the back porch engrossed in an intense game of Candy Land. Maddie looked up, smiled, and whispered, "I'm losing, *again!*"

Callie laughed and collapsed into one of the chairs.

"How was the service?"

"It was really nice," Callie responded. "There were so many people, they had to set chairs up outside!"

Maddie smiled. "I'm not surprised."

Callie nodded toward Henry. "How's he doing?"

"He's doing very well. He has won the last three games. Somehow, I keep landing on those black dots and then I'm stuck there forever."

"I don't think I ever tried playing a board game with him."

"Well, it took him a little while to get used to taking turns." Henry looked up, waiting for Maddie to go, and she drew a card and moved. "But he understands now. Taking turns can sometimes be a hard lesson for kids with autism, but games like this are good practice for developing all kinds of social skills. He also helped me make peanut butter and jelly sandwiches for lunch, *and* we drew some pictures." Maddie paused. "Henry likes to draw animals and, in particular, one special dog." She looked questioningly at Callie.

Callie smiled and said, "That must be Springer." At the mention of Springer's name, Henry looked up, and Callie said, "Springer's not here, Henry." After that, Henry lost interest in the game.

"Would you rather draw, Henry?" Maddie asked, sliding the pad and pencil and a new box of crayons over to him. Henry pushed the game away, picked up the pencil, opened to a new page, and began to draw, and Maddie looked back at Callie. "Springer must be pretty special."

Callie nodded. "He *is*. He's Linden's dog, and they are pretty attached."

"Is he the one that stayed with Henry that night?"

Callie nodded, wondering how Maddie knew.

"You should always try to encourage a special bond like that, if possible. Anything that Henry seems to show interest in or a fondness for should be encouraged and nourished."

Callie nodded, and Maddie smiled. "I really enjoyed spending time with Henry today. He's very bright, Callie, so don't get discouraged. In fact, I think he'd be a wonderful candidate for the new Excel program we're starting in the elementary school." She stood to go, lightly touched Henry's arm, and waved. "Bye, Henry. I had fun today." Henry looked up from his drawing and opened and closed his small fist.

54

As the summer days slipped by, Callie was surprised by the warm strength she felt in facing life's challenges. She still missed her dad desperately and often struggled in tearful despair over his loss, but she found solace in the words he'd shared with her about his faith: *No matter what trials you're facing, Cal, God gives you the strength to get through them.* And she had come to believe it was true. She also found that she felt closer to him when she was working in his garden, especially if a hummingbird buzzed by like a navy pilot giving her a flyby. One morning when she was pulling weeds she unearthed a small wooden sign that her dad had made when she was little. She gently brushed off the dirt and read the once familiar words: YOU CAN'T GET IN TROUBLE WHEN YOU'RE WEEDING! The wisdom of it still rang true.

Henry also enjoyed working in the garden. Callie discovered that quiet, methodical activities soothed him, and weeding was one of them. He would follow her out to the garage to retrieve the old bushel her dad had always used and then march off into the sunshine with it banging against his short legs. *How lucky,* Callie thought, *to have a child that likes weeding!*

She also discovered he had a mischievous

streak. On hot days, she would help him into his bathing suit, set him up with the hose, and go back to weeding. Moments later she'd be bent down in the hot sun and feel cold water showering down on her back. She'd look up in time to see Henry look away, suppressing a grin.

The garden had two long, winding beds filled with bee balm, black-eyed Susan, echinacea, lilies of every color, and blue and purple hydrangeas. There was also a separate bed for herbs: chives, parsley, basil, and tarragon. The last bed had always been reserved for vegetables, and even though it was late in the season, Callie had found four scraggly beefsteak tomato plants and one wilted cherry tomato plant at Agway. She'd bought them at a significant discount, brought them home, planted and watered them, and showed Henry how to pluck off the suckers that sprouted in the crooks between the trunk and branches. Henry took his new job seriously, and any potential suckers never grew more than a half an inch before Henry pinched them off. He was also very intrigued by the abundant clusters of little green balls on the cherry tomato plant and checked them daily when they started to change color. Finally, when they ripened to a bright fire engine red, Callie showed him how to pluck them from the vine and pop them, warm and sweet, right into his mouth.

On rainy days, Callie worked inside. One of the

first projects she took on was turning her old bedroom into a bedroom for Henry. She boxed up all of her trophies, moved out her furniture, stripped off the faded wallpaper, puttied and sanded the walls, and let Henry pick out a new color. After the walls had two coats of fresh paint, she moved her old bed and dresser back in but rearranged them so the bed was against the wall and there was room for Henry's old shelf and a small desk that she found in the garage. Finally, Callie surprised him with a new set of John Deere tractor sheets and, the first night they were on his bed, she had no trouble getting him *in* bed!

Callie talked to Henry constantly and explained everything she did. They read books, played games, and tried to stick to a schedule that Henry could count on. Gradually, he began to use words more frequently, and to Callie it seemed as if an evil spell had been broken. In the beginning, Henry just repeated words and sayings that he heard on TV, and she sometimes heard him whispering to himself, as if trying the words out: *"What's up, doc?"* or *"Sheriff, this is no time to panic."* These were two of his favorites, but slowly he began to express himself and converse too.

Maddie was very interested in hearing every detail of Henry's progress. Even though he still had moments of frustration and occasional temper tantrums, the frequency of these diminished as his ability to communicate increased. At Maddie's suggestion, Callie filled out the registration for the new program at the elementary school, and in late August, she and Henry visited the classroom. When they arrived, Maddie was busy hanging red paper apples on the bulletin board, but she stopped to show Henry his desk, and invited him to hang the apple with his name on it on the brown paper tree. Callie watched him reach up and hang it from one of the lowest branches. She was thrilled for him. Not only would he be able to come to this warm, welcoming place every day, but he would be taught by a wonderful, understanding teacher who was quickly becoming a dear friend.

Callie also told Maddie about her hope to go back to school, too, and Maddie suggested she consider Keene State. Right after Callie dropped Henry off on his first day, she drove to the campus and registered for a morning class that would put her on the path to finishing her degree and getting her teaching certificate in special education. She couldn't wait to tell Maddie the news.

55

When Linden returned the pilot's headset, Fairbanks looked surprised and asked how Henry was doing. Linden answered that he thought he was doing better but then he quickly changed the subject, and Fairbanks, sensing Linden didn't want to talk about it, didn't ask again.

The summer days slipped by and Linden made steady progress on the old wall. Sometimes, when he was leaving for the day, he'd see Fairbanks standing on the porch, holding up two cold beer bottles and smiling. They'd sit on the porch, talk about the world's problems, and listen to the melancholy chirring of the cicadas high up in the trees. By mid-September, however, the cool evening air whispered of autumn and the only sound that drifted from the woods was the occasional tentative chirp of a chilly cricket.

In a vain attempt to push Callie from his mind, Linden also began running again. He even retired his old Prefontaine racers and invested in a new pair of Nike trainers. Every morning, as soon as the sun was up, he headed out. In the beginning, Kat and Springer loped along beside him but, after he began putting in eighty miles a week, he decided that it would be better if they stayed home.

The only thing that changed in the barnyard that fall was the little bull's size. He was, already, almost as big as his mother. With Cindy's blessing, Linden had named him Robert, after his favorite poet, and because he thought he should keep the "R" theme going.

Linden finally finished the wall in early October, and Fairbanks insisted on taking him to dinner. They went to Harlow's, and it dawned on Linden that he hadn't been there since he'd had dinner with Callie and Henry. They sat in the bar, and Linden ordered two beers but Fairbanks stopped him and said he felt like a nip of juniper juice. Linden raised his eyebrows and Fairbanks chuckled. "It's my autumn drink." So they ordered gin and tonics, steaming bowls of clam chowder, and Reubens. While they sipped their drinks and waited for their food, Fairbanks told Linden he would be heading back to the city for the winter and added that he hoped Linden might be willing to look after the house and keep the driveway plowed when it snowed. Linden was surprised; he hadn't thought about his friend leaving, but he agreed to look after the house, and Fairbanks reached into his pocket and presented him with a key. He also told Linden that he planned to have a big Christmas party at the house in December, and he hoped Linden would come *and* bring a date! Linden said he would definitely come, but he couldn't promise he'd have a date. At that, Fairbanks took off his glasses, wiped them with his flannel shirt, and said, "You need someone, my boy, to keep you warm out here in these rugged New England winters."

Linden nodded and, with a sad smile, said, "Maybe, someday. . . ."

56

On the day before Thanksgiving, Callie picked Henry up from school and they made a special trip to Windy Hill Orchard to buy apples. As they drove, she thought of all the times she and her dad had gone apple picking together. One time, they'd gotten up extra early to get more apples for the pies her mom was making for the church fair. When they'd parked in the field, it was still shrouded in morning mist and the old farmer was just coming out of the house with a cup of coffee. She and her dad had slogged through the long grass, heavy with dew, carrying large bags, and in no time at all, Callie's sneakers and socks had become soggy and squishy. The gnarled old boughs of the trees had rested on the ground, groaning under the weight of their abundant fruit. But what Callie remembered most about that trip was looking down through the misty orchard and seeing a herd of deer walking through the trees, munching contentedly on the sweet apples. She and her dad had stood and watched for a long time and, when they'd finally returned home with the apples, her mom had said, "My goodness! I was getting ready to send out a search party!"

It was too late in the season to pick apples this year, but maybe next year they would find time to go. *The little tomato farmer would certainly enjoy picking apples!* They went into the gift shop and Callie bought a half-peck of Macs and a gallon of cider. On their way out, Henry spied a small toy John Deere tractor, and Callie gave in and bought that too.

After supper that night, Callie pulled out her mom's tattered *Good Housekeeping* cookbook and looked up the recipe for piecrusts. Then she searched through her mom's recipe box for the stained and faded card on which her mom's apple pie filling was neatly printed. Callie studied the card, remembered that her mom's secret ingredient was red cinnamon candy, and looked in the spice cabinet, hoping. She moved around the small jars and tins and finally found a small container with about a tablespoon left of the little red hearts. *Just enough!*

While she rolled out the piecrust, she listened to the familiar program Henry was watching in the living room. Lucy was trying to trick Charlie Brown into thinking she was going to let him kick the football. "Don't believe her," Callie whispered. "She can't be trusted!" A moment later, Callie heard a loud *AAUGH!* followed by a painful thud. She shook her head in dismay. "I warned you, Charlie Brown!" She continued to listen to the classic sounds the adults made as Charlie Brown talked to his grandmother on the phone. Then she heard the Peanuts gang belting out "Over the River and Through the Woods," and pretty soon Henry trundled into the kitchen, repeating the nasal sound, "Mwa, mwa-mwa, mwa mwa-mwa." Callie laughed, and Henry smiled shyly.

"Want some apple slices?" Callie asked.

Henry nodded and she put some slices in a small bowl. Henry took the bowl and carefully put it on the table and then pushed a chair over to the counter to open the cabinet where they kept the peanut butter. Callie stopped peeling and watched him. He took out the peanut butter, hopped down, got a spoon from the drawer, dropped a big glob of peanut butter into the bowl with the apples, took an apple slice, dunked it into the peanut butter, and, licking the peanut butter, wandered back into the living room. Callie resumed peeling and shook her head. *Where in the world did he learn that?*

She added sugar, cinnamon, nutmeg, and a dash of salt to the apples and stirred everything together in a big bowl. Then she filled the uncooked piecrust with the apple mixture and strategically placed a dozen or so of the tiny red candy hearts on top of the filling. Gingerly, she slid a spatula around under the rolled-out dough that was still adhered to the counter, rolled it deftly onto her rolling pin so it draped over both sides, held the roller so it wouldn't spin, and laid the top crust gently over the apples. She pressed and pinched the two crusts together, making a decorative pattern. Then she cut a small piece of extra dough into the shape of an apple and leaf and laid the pieces on top. She dipped her fingers in a little milk and lightly coated the top crust with it. Finally, she made a long aluminum foil shield to protect the crust, wrapped it around the pie's circumference, and slid the pie into the hot oven.

"There," she said softly, "I did it, Mom . . . and I didn't even cry."

Henry wandered into the kitchen with his empty bowl, and Callie said, "You are just the man I wanted to see. It's bedtime!" This news was met with some resistance, but no more than any little boy would give.

57

Linden fell asleep on the couch watching Jay Leno and woke up with a kink in his neck. He leaned forward, rubbing it. "How come we didn't go to bed two hours ago?" he mumbled to the dogs sprawled in front of the fireplace. At the sound of his voice they opened their eyes and thumped their tails. "Do you two need to go out?" he asked. They both got up sleepily, stretched, and wandered over to the door. Linden let them out and stood on the porch, shivering. "Make it quick!"

Ten minutes later he was lying in bed, wide awake. *Maybe I should just skip the race tomorrow,* he thought. But then he remembered that he'd told his dad he wasn't coming for dinner because he was running in a race, so he rolled over, set his alarm, and pulled the quilt up to his chin. He'd been trying to get by without turning on the furnace. Last year, he'd made it all the way to Thanksgiving Day, but he'd heard it was going to warm up over the weekend, so maybe he could break his old record.

He had just begun to doze off when Springer, who was lying against the bed, began snoring loudly and Linden reached over to shake him. The hapless yellow Lab snorted, stretched, and rolled onto his back with all four legs straight up in the air. "Forget it," Linden grumbled. "It's too late for a belly rub." But Springer kept his position and began snoring so loudly that Linden had to pull his pillow over his head.

Callie stayed up late watching *The Tonight Show* while she waited for the pie to bake, so she was surprised when she woke up early on Thanksgiving morning. She sighed, pushed off her quilt, reached for her flannel robe, peeked in on Henry, and slipped quietly to the kitchen to make coffee. While she waited for it to brew, she looked at the pie and could almost hear her mom's voice *It looks like a picture!* She'd thought about making a pumpkin pie too, but then decided there was no way she and Henry could eat two pies. Maybe she'd make one next week, when this one was gone. In the meantime, she still had dinner to think about. Her heart really wasn't in making a big dinner, but she'd already bought a small turkey, stuffing, dried apricots, cranberry sauce, sweet potatoes, and vegetables. She had no idea when, or if, she'd have time to make everything, but she wanted Henry to know the fun of Thanksgiving traditions, even if it was just the two of them.

Callie poured steaming coffee into her dad's mug, took a sip, and went down the hall to take a quick shower. The first thing she wanted to do after breakfast was visit the cemetery.

Linden slept fitfully and woke up several times during the night. Finally, he gave up, pulled on his faded Levis and flannel shirt, and shuffled to the kitchen to make coffee. While it brewed cheerfully, he let the dogs out, switched on the radio, and looked out the kitchen window at the cold gray river. WGBH happened to be coming in and the program host was introducing the next song.

"The original composition, 'Simple Gifts,' was written by Elder Joseph Brackett in 1848 while he was at a Shaker community in Alfred, Maine. It's often called a hymn or a work song, but these descriptions are inaccurate, as it is really a dance. The recording I'm going to play is by the New

251

York Philharmonic with Leonard Bernstein conducting. I know we are well into autumn, so I hope you will forgive me; here now is Appalachian Spring.*"*

Linden listened to the familiar recording of the beautiful suite and wondered if his parents were listening too. His mother, he imagined, had her apron on and was probably "dressing the bird," as his father called it. "A twenty-pounder," he'd exclaimed, trying to convince Linden to make the trip, but Linden had declined. He had no interest in discussing politics or religion, and he definitely didn't want to listen to his mother ask him when he was going to get a real job.

He poured steaming coffee into his faded lighthouse mug, took a sip, let the dogs in, fed them, and then pulled on his boots and barn coat and took his coffee out to the barn to feed the rest of the animals. The Turkey Trot was at nine, so if he was going, he'd better get his chores out of the way.

After the breakfast dishes were cleaned up, Callie bundled Henry into his new jacket. Two weeks earlier, she'd helped him into the old blue one he'd worn last year and his wrists had stuck out two inches past the end of the sleeves. "Wow, Henry, I guess you grew!" she'd exclaimed in surprise. She zipped up his new jacket, and he marched over to the door. When they stepped outside, though, she couldn't believe how mild it was and she wondered if he needed a jacket at all. She went back in the house and grabbed his sweatshirt too.

Linden laced up his trainers and looked around. There was a pretty good turnout for Thanksgiving morning. Most of the runners were enjoying the Indian summer weather and had donned shorts and T-shirts for the event. Linden pinned his number to his faded Dartmouth singlet. They lined up for the start and, although Linden harbored no hopes of winning, he lined up near a group of shirtless high school boys who looked like they might be part of the local cross-country team. *This could be fun,* he thought as he stretched.

A moment later, the horn sounded, and they were off. The group of boys seemed determined to lead, so Linden let them go, but when they hit the first hill he began picking them off one by one. *Not bad for an old guy!* They crested the hill, and Linden picked up his pace. He was surprised at how strong he felt. They passed the first mile mark, and he glanced at his watch: *5:25. You can do better than that!* Up a long incline, he passed two more hotshots, and then he began to wonder how many runners were actually ahead of him. He thought there was at least one, but he couldn't see anyone. Finally, when he topped the last hill, he spotted the lead runner two hundred meters ahead.

This one's for you, Cal! He focused on the boy's back and picked up his pace, hoping his young competitor wouldn't look back. Steadily, he began closing the gap *and* began to feel like he was back in high school. One hundred meters, fifty meters, thirty meters. *Step lightly or he'll hear you!* With twenty meters to go and the finish line in sight, the boy finally glanced over his shoulder and realized he had company. Meanwhile, the sleepy crowd woke up and realized there was a race going on! An explosion of cheering erupted along both sides of the road. Linden's muscles burned but, with fifteen meters to go, he was right behind him, and at ten they were neck and neck! When they were side by side, Linden began to wonder if his lungs might explode. But finally, with three meters to go, the boy dug deep and pulled a step ahead.

"Good race!" he said, coming back breathlessly to shake Linden's hand.

Linden straightened up from trying to catch his breath, shook the boy's outstretched hand. "Yes, good race!"

"Did you go to Dartmouth?" the boy asked, nodding to Linden's singlet.

"A long time ago," Linden said, wiping his face with it.

"Well, good race! I win the turkey, but your prize is better. . . . You win the pumpkin pie!" Linden nodded and smiled. He hadn't known there were prizes.

58

Callie turned into the cemetery and parked near the road. She helped Henry climb out and he stopped to gaze at the rows of headstones. He remembered this place. He remembered these white and gray stones sticking out of the ground, and he remembered leaving a small smooth rock on top of one of them.

Callie followed Henry through the maze of old graves and was surprised when he remembered the way. They came to the familiar shady knoll, protected by pine trees, and Henry frowned: There were two stones now! He walked over to the new one and stood in front of it. Then he ran his hand over the top and lightly traced the letters:

BENJAMIN FRANKLIN WYETH
JANUARY 22, 1947–JULY 9, 1999
DEAR HUSBAND ~
BELOVED FATHER & GRANDFATHER
HONORED VETERAN ~ FAITHFUL FRIEND

Callie fought back her tears. *Why does it have to be this way? Why can't they be here to share the holidays with us? Why weren't they given lives that included knowing their grandson and watching him grow up?* She knelt down on the soft bed of pine needles that surrounded the graves and suddenly caught her breath. Two beautiful white lilies were growing up between the headstones. *This isn't the time of year for lilies,* she thought. *How in the world have they survived the cold?* She watched as Henry searched the ground for a second suitable stone. When he found it, he turned and carefully placed it on top of her dad's headstone, and then something caught his eye and he looked up the hill behind her. "Who cooks for you?" he said softly.

Callie stood, turned to follow his gaze, and saw Linden walking toward them.

"Hey," he said, drawing closer.

"Hey," she said, brushing away her tears and smiling.

"I was driving by and I saw that old Nova parked near the road." He paused. "I hope it's okay that I stopped."

She nodded. "Of course! What are you doing up this way?"

"I was running in the Turkey Trot."

She smiled. "Did you win?"

Linden shook his head. "I came in second. First place won a turkey, but second place," he said with a grin, "won a pumpkin pie!"

"You won a pumpkin pie?"

Linden nodded proudly.

"Punkin pie," Henry whispered from where he was standing near the headstone. Linden smiled and knelt down. "Henry, did you just say *punkin pie?*" Henry nodded, and Linden laughed and put out his hand. "Can you give me five?" Henry walked over shyly and slapped his hand down on Linden's. "Thanks!" Linden said, ruffling his hair.

Henry nodded and whispered, "Sheriff, this is no time to panic."

Linden gave Callie a puzzled look, but she just shrugged and shook her head. "I think it's from a movie. . . ."

Linden nodded. "It's really great that he's talking." He paused. "How have you been?"

Callie smiled. "I'm managing. Coming here always makes me sad, but that's okay. How 'bout you?"

"I'm managing too," he said. "Life's pretty quiet."

"How are the animals?"

"They're fine. That calf is getting big."

Callie hesitated. "Linden, I'm sure you probably already have plans . . ." she began uncertainly.

Linden searched her eyes and slowly shook his head. "No, I don't have plans."

"You're not having turkey?"

He shook his head again. "You can't really cook a turkey for one person."

Callie smiled. "I know. You can't really cook a turkey for one and a half people either, but I was going to try." She hesitated again. "Listen, if you're really not doing anything, would you like to have Thanksgiving with us?"

Linden smiled and nodded. "I'd like that."

Henry slipped his hand into Callie's and softly whispered Springer's name, and Linden knelt down in front of him. "Springer likes turkey too. Do you think I should bring him?"

Henry nodded, looking up at Callie for approval, and she knelt down next to him. "Do you think Linden should bring Kat too?"

Henry smiled shyly and nodded again.

As they walked up the hill, Callie whispered something in Henry's ear, and he looked over at Linden and said, "Don't forget the punkin pie!"

Linden laughed. "Oh, I won't! I think that's why your mom invited me!"

Epilogue

Callie heard the vacuum in the hallway outside her classroom, glanced up at the clock, and realized it was getting late. She lifted Sam's chair back onto his desk, slipped her books and papers into her canvas bag, pulled on her coat, and walked toward the door. As she reached up to turn off the lights a poster hanging next to the door caught her eye. It had an image of a blue puzzle piece in the center and underneath were printed the words "Autism Speaks. . . . It's time to listen." Callie had walked past the poster hundreds of times, but this time she paused to reflect on how far the world had come in its awareness and understanding of autism. She smiled and thought, *Henry has come a long way too!* Just then, Jim came around the corner with his vacuum and waved. Callie waved back and left the lights on for him.

Ten minutes later, she parked her new Subaru Outback behind the high school, got out, and buttoned her barn coat as she hurried across the parking lot. She couldn't believe it was November already. *Where has the time gone?* It seemed as if the school year had just started and now Thanksgiving was just around the corner. She reached into her pocket for her fleece hat, pulled it down over her ears, and hoped that Henry had remembered his hat too. She looked across the playing fields at the small crowd gathering under the gray New Hampshire sky. As she hurried to join them, she felt her heart pounding with anticipation and excitement. She slipped through the crowd and discovered that the boys were already lining up. "Good luck, Hen-Ben!" she called. A slender boy wearing a bright orange hat looked over and smiled, and Callie smiled back, her eyes brimming with thankful tears.

"Hey," a familiar voice said behind her.

Callie turned, and Linden gave her a hello kiss.

"They haven't started yet?" he asked.

"Nope, you're just in time."

"Good! I was sure I was going to miss it."

An official standing near the starting line held up his air horn and shouted, "All ready?" One breath later, the horn blasted through the New Hampshire countryside and the boys were off, up the hill and into the woods. Callie and Linden watched them go and then hurried with the rest of the parents to the next viewing area. As they stood waiting, straining to see them come out of the woods, the late-day sun dropped below the clouds and stretched bright rays of sunlight across the fields. Callie shielded her eyes and held her breath, praying, and then spotted Henry's famous orange hat.

"There's Henry Finch!" someone yelled.

"Go, Henry!" Linden shouted.

Cheering voices filled the air, and someone exclaimed, "Wow! That boy can fly!" Henry rounded the corner, putting more and more distance between himself and the field of boys behind him, and Callie blinked back tears and whispered, "Look, Dad, here comes our boy!"

As Henry ran past, she shouted, "Go get 'em, kiddo! You can do it!"

DISCUSSION QUESTIONS

1. Callie struggles with feelings of guilt and remorse and even wonders if Henry's autism is punishment for her indiscretion. Do you think sin triggers punishment, and does God make bad things happen?

2. Callie is a "type A" personality. She is competitive and sometimes self-centered. How does she change?

3. In what ways does Linden's personality differ from Callie's? Does their relationship give credence to the old adage "Opposites attract"?

4. One of Callie's best attributes is that she thoughtfully considers the counsel of others. What are some examples of this and how do these words of wisdom help Callie grow?

5. Throughout the story, Callie fondly remembers childhood moments with her dad and, even though his death is devastating, she finds the strength to carry on. How does her dad's faith help Callie learn to face life's trials?

6. Fairbanks, Dr. Franklin, and Maddie all play similar roles in the story. What are their roles and why are they similar?

7. What role do the animals play in the story?

8. Callie's screen door is an important element in the story. What are some of the events that mention the door? Who are the people who knock on Callie's door or visit the house? What is the reason for each one's visit?

9. Callie, Linden, and Henry all have obstacles to overcome. What are the obstacles each one faces and how do they overcome them?

10. How has the awareness and understanding of autism changed in recent years?

Center Point Large Print
600 Brooks Road / PO Box 1
Thorndike ME 04986-0001 USA

(207) 568-3717

US & Canada:
1 800 929-9108
www.centerpointlargeprint.com